C000243649

Contents

Against a Sea of Troubles

JJD Thomas

ISBN: 979-8-9897602-0-6

eBook ISBN: 979-8-9897602-1-3

Book Cover by S. Monroe

Preface

Please do not burn this book.

I understand that I am a criminal—a murderer and a pirate—and, beyond criminal, I am a blasphemer, who consorts with sorcerers and demons. Even so, I beseech an open mind. Yes, in someone else's story, my love and I might be villains, but in this one we are heroes, even if only to each other. We both chose cursed lives over shackles, and, by being companion to one another, we were able to turn that evil to good. Much like how one magpie is an omen for sorrow, but two is an omen for mirth; alone, I was miserable and hopeless, but once I met another like me and saw what he made of his ill fortune, then I found the power to free myself.

If you are trapped as I was trapped, as Toussaint was trapped, then I want this book to be your second magpie. I want you to read my story of escape and see that it is possible. If all you see is sorrow and darkness in your future, let this be your first company. Bad fortune and tragic fates are our enemies. Let us fight those destinies together.

Your Fellow Bad Omen,
Mariah Goldenleaf

One for Sorrow

When the pirate known as "Bad Weather" was loaded onto the *Triton*, I did not at first give him a thought. I was lost in my own melancholy: staring out at the sea, with one arm draped over the rail, fingers stretched down to catch stray drops as they leapt from sapphire surf. We were to take the pirate to Port Royal, where he would face justice at the end of a rope, but as I also considered myself to be heading towards the end of my life, I did not spare him my sympathy. This is the nature of melancholy. I felt the fate of my unhappy marriage as heavy on my shoulders as a set of stocks, and that weight pressed down my head onto my arm onto the side of the boat. I felt such a cold, hollow sorrow in my heart as I wondered why it was that I was alive at all, and how much silence and cold, boring nothingness awaited me in this new world. I was sad, but as this is a story of pirates, let us not dwell on it.

The port officers of Antigua had a somber cloud of guilt about them when they loaded Bad Weather onto our ship. The pirate, known by some as Toussaint Dupuis, had a horrible reputation for bad luck. It was said that to go to sea with him was the same as pointing one's bow into a tempest. The officers suspected that whichever unlucky vessel was meant to take the pirate to his hanging would be swallowed up by the sea long before it arrived, and their guilt made them confess this news before leaving us. Bad Weather himself corroborated these stories, with much self-effacing, and in such a matter-of-fact, good-natured way as to say, this is my lot in life and I've accepted it.

Having a bad omen on board set the men to bickering. Sailors are a superstitious lot by nature; it doesn't matter how many things go right on a voyage, for one hole in a hull will sink the ship. They tried to reassure each other, saying that it was only a short journey to Jamaica, and besides, if this Frenchman was going to his hanging, then wouldn't it be bad luck for *him* if the journey went well? And this last argument received many nods and hearty clappings of backs, but, even so, a persistent aura of unease haunted this leg of the voyage, and many eyes kept shooting upwards to the sky to see whether the weather seemed likely to turn sour.

Bad Weather himself was in high spirits. There was no place on our heavily laden merchant vessel to store a captive, so the captain secured him to the forward mast to keep an eye on him. There, the pirate attempted to make conversation with the crew, without much success. I could see him from my post in the back, always smiling and laughing at his own jokes, trying to make the stony-faced sailors crack. He found little purchase in those around him, but I, on the other hand, was already a little charmed from afar.

Even in my melancholy (which was pervasive, and quite dampened my soul), I found myself sickened with curiosity about the young pirate. How was someone with such an ugly reputation, and on such an ill-fated journey, still in high spirits? Besides, he was far too beautiful to be a pirate. He wore his hair in a thick, black mane, which the wind and seawater only ever seemed to thicken with waves, and though his

3

chin was clean-shaven, his eyebrows were as sharp and finely plucked as those of a French madame. On the second day he was with us, I took my ocean-staring down to his side of the ship in order to better hear him talk. If I'm being honest, I watched him more than was proper for a woman engaged, but as I was soon to be married off to a stranger twice my age and forever locked inside a lonely hermitage, then right now was the time to bear the risk of being a little immodest.

"What do you think of?" he asked me, "When you're looking out at the ocean?"

My heart jumped up into my throat. I hadn't spoken to him. At that moment, I was simply doing my best not to stare, and, in truth, what I was thinking about was him.

"Nothing at all," I answered without looking up from the sea.

"Oh, come now, mademoiselle," he teased, his French accent buzzing. "You think I'll believe you to be thoughtless? I can see something moving under your eyes. It appears to me to be a great tragedy at work." The man's accent was French, but he spoke English with great fluency. "Come, share your tragedy with me. We can commiserate. You know that I'm in for one myself."

I didn't want to talk about my tragedy. I was only a bookbinder's daughter, about to marry above my station, and, despite all my woolgathering, I did not really understand why my match to the governor of Jamaica made me miserable. My father said that I was lucky to find anyone who would marry a sickly and old hermit of a girl who spent all of her time indoors, and, although I didn't think that he was wrong, I couldn't feel lucky about it.

I asked him instead, "Then why do you seem so merry?"

Bad Weather flashed a disarming smile at me, and said, "I have good company, do I not?" but I was not disarmed, and he elaborated. "I am a man oft accompanied by misery. If I always drug my company into

4

that misery with me, why, I'd never have any friends, and that would be a misfortune far greater than anything my demon of bad luck could inflict upon me."

I frowned, more in thought than in rebuke. "So you really do think that you're bad luck."

"Do you doubt it? I am the greatest sailor of storms in all the Caribbean, thanks to the practice fate has blessed me with, again and again and again."

"I'm not a superstitious person, generally," I said, "But to be honest, it's more that I don't know how much to trust what you say. You're very long-spoken for a pirate."

"Really?" he laughed. "Am I not well-spoken?"

"Maybe that too. But you are a man of many words, and in my experience, people like that can't fill every one of their many words with honest meaning. They fill half with boasts and lies and flatterings. So how do I know what is truth and what is boast?"

Rather than be unhappy with my calling him a liar (in a roundabout way), Bad Weather seemed pleased with me for saying so. He shook his head with a smile on his face, like we were playing a game of words.

"Mademoiselle," he said. "I entertain a number of shortcomings, I assure you, but you have not chosen one of them. There is so much to the world to talk about. You say that I have many words, but they only flitter around the meaning of the world without really capturing it. I am a poet, not by trade but by temperament, and I assure you that the truth of the world goes much deeper than what I can catch. I am aware of my short-falling, despite wishing more than anything to hold a bit of the beauty of the world in my mouth. I wish to tell a blind man what it feels like to look upon the sea, but have never found the words. Yet I do try in earnest, I assure you of that."

"So you're a poet, not a pirate?" I asked with a wry twist to my words.

"I can be both things. You could also call me a sailor or a gambler or a man of bad decisions, and all would be equally correct."

"And a braggart and a knave?"

"A man may be a cosmos, and even your cruel names stars."

"Yet you would rather I see the poet than the pirate."

"Aye, but only because we may have different understandings of piracy."

"Oh indeed? Do you think it a noble pursuit?"

I was leaning forward, and smiling, for the first time in a long and dull voyage. I leaned in to better hear his musical accent and the dancing of his words around themselves, but that leaning attracted the captain's attention, and he lumbered down to break us apart.

"Don't be filling the lady's head with tripe," Captain Peterson growled, laying a heavy hand upon my shoulder. He was a very large, older man, nearing the end of his seafaring career. It was his job to keep me safe on the way to my husband, and he saw all men as my predators. He had threatened the crew not to speak a word more than necessary to me throughout the voyage, out of some puritan fear of Eve's fickle character, and their fear of him had stayed the course.

"It's all proper, uncle," I mumbled. I tried to tug my shoulder out from under his hand, but it was too heavy. He wasn't my real uncle; he was just an old friend of my father. The two of them would meet up and drink together in silence whenever he was in town, and apparently that counted as friendship among such men.

"'Tis not 'proper,'" Peterson said, pointing an accusatory finger at the pirate. "That is not the way that a gentleman looks at a lady."

Bad Weather smiled like an imp, and he sounded like he was trying to hold in a laugh when he said, "My *lady*, I'm sorry for the deceit—it's not in my nature to lie—but I am not at all a gentleman."

Something about the way he said it at the end gave me goosebumps and incensed my uncle into a quiet kind of rage.

"No, you're a dead man," he said coldly, "and there's no use in talking to one."

Uncle Peterson jerked me away from the pirate, heading back towards the helm, but Bad Weather interrupted us before we'd gone three steps.

"Captain," the pirate piped up. "A storm will be hitting us around evening. You should take us to moor off of Hispaniola to wait it out."

Peterson sneered back over his shoulder. He was taller than most men and towered over the restrained pirate. "So your French *amis* can ambush us? Eh? No, we're going straight away to the gallows, pirate. You won't be wiggling your way out of this one."

"Do you have storm sails?" Bad Weather asked, unshaken. "You'll need to start putting them up soon if you plan on continuing..."

The captain pulled me away, grumbling down to me, "Don't be listening to him, Mariah. A pirate's a pirate, and he'll say what he has to."

The rest of the pirate's warnings were swallowed up by the waves.

I spared a glance backwards as I was marched up the stair onto the back deck. Toussaint seemed worried, but I didn't trust myself to judge whether his worry was genuine. I didn't trust myself to do anything, as a rule, and certainly not to go against the orders of my uncle, who warned me against saying anything else to the pirate for as long as he lived. I nodded at his warnings and returned to staring off of the back of the boat.

My habit at that point in my life, when confronted with any decision or force of the world, was to freeze. I stayed quiet and went along with whatever caused the least trouble for everyone around me. That's how I ended up on a ship to the Caribbean to meet and marry an old man: it was best for my father and my uncle and ostensibly for me, a spinster at twenty years old, to accept the match and ship off. I did have yearnings of my own, and I had dreams; I had lusts and rages and hungers—but I buried them all in the heavy rime of obedience, so that they only tickled at the underside of my heart rather than taking it over. I would rather freeze than cause trouble, at least back then.

Whether it was truly Bad Weather's knowledge of storms, or perhaps a more preternatural sense, the sky appeared to be following his predictions by the end of the afternoon. Low, gray clouds overtook the blue until there was scarcely a shred of color left in the sky. These nomadic harbingers of bad weather brought grumbling to the sailors of the *Triton*, who as a group all grew increasingly discontented as the hours passed and the clouds darkened without abatement.

"Perhaps we should find a shore to wait out the storm, Captain," First Mate Anderson said, tugging nervously on the brim of his cap as he came up to the wheel. "It looks like this is going to get worse afore it gets better."

"We continue to Port Royal," Captain Peterson ordered.

"If we turn 'round we can make Hispaniola in an hour," Anderson pressed again, "But even if we do, we'll be in rain afore landfall. If the Mister Toussaint is to be believed..."

"'Mister?'" Peterson growled. "Devil rot that 'Mister.' You can't be letting a little superstition make the sky look darker than it is. It'll be a rain, but we'll be in port by tomorrow if I have anything to say about it." He withdrew his brandy flask from his coat and spun the cap off. "'Mister.' Bah." he muttered and took a deep draught.

My uncle was a stubborn man, and on any ordinary day, he was loath to change plans. When doing so required that he accept the word of a pirate, there was no chance of it. These plans included the captain's habit of being drunk by evening, which was in his plan for every day. His flask was running low earlier than usual, and he was inside, filling it back up from his barrel of brandy, when the rain hit.

The rain was shockingly cold and made a sound like hail when it hit the deck. The captain came out of his cabin to find sailors huddling under sails, looking up with horror as if the apocalypse itself were upon them.

"Lower the sails, dammit!" Captain Peterson shouted at them. "Then wait out the rain below, and if any of you swine shows your snout above deck afore morning, I'll have you keelhauled for insubordination." Then he returned inside to drink.

Bad Weather tried to catch the sailors' attention as they followed the captain's orders, but they were in a hurry to make the *Triton* ready for rain, and none gave him their ears.

"It's going to get worse," he warned. "You need to keep the jib up, sail with the wind. You cannot leave your fate up to the storms in this sea or they will toss you up out of them."

I heard only this much before Anderson seized me by the wrist and brought me back to the captain's cabin.

The *Triton* only had one cabin. It was usually reserved for the captain, but he had me share with him to keep me away from the other sailors. The captain drank in silence, and the brandy made for a buffer around his ears, so that as the rainfall worsened, he fell further into unconsciousness, until finally the flask dropped from his hand onto the deck below.

We bobbed on the water like a turtle with its head in its shell, knowing that we were at the mercy of the tempest, but hoping to

9

survive by hunkering. There was nothing more to do—the time for mutiny had passed, and now whether we crashed or not was up to luck. Every minute that I spent waiting, tapping my foot and looking worriedly out the window, the storm worsened. The wood began to creak, and every time a wave smashed against the back of our ship, I felt sure that this was the one that would crush it to splinters. As worried as I was for myself, I was more so for the pirate tied to our mast, who had no shell to hide in. Before, my melancholy at my own trap and my own helplessness had kept me from thinking of his sorrow, but now the reality of his helplessness, and all the ways that he could be crushed or punctured or otherwise injured without any hope of defending himself, made my own fears feel weak.

Once I saw my uncle's flask drop, I made up my mind. It wasn't an easy thing to do. I was still a dreadful coward, having had no practice yet at going against my fears. I did not feel decisive as I stared at my uncle's cutlass on its hook, urging my hand to raise and take action. The bucking of the boat made me stumble face-first into the hanging sheathe, and once I had it in my hands, there was only the door between me and the storm. The force of the winds made it impossible to open, and I worried that a crate had shifted in front of the door. I jumped into it with all my weight until finally it opened up to the true sound of the storm beyond.

The wind was blowing so powerfully that it made the rain fall sideways. It felt like a sheet of needles on my skin and hit the deck so hard that the droplets burst into mists that flew around like vengeful ghosts. Bad Weather was still tied to the mast, and he was alive. I could see him shouting up at the storm like a man possessed, though I couldn't begin to hear his taunts over the roaring of the gale. My uncle was wrong about that at least: this was much more than a little rain.

The deck bucked underneath me as I crossed it, and I flew/fell into the pirate's mast, colliding against him and grabbing hold of the ropes that held him there. He stared at me with a sudden, wide-eyed fear.

"What are you doing?" he asked.

In answer, I drew the sword. I stood back, and even though I wobbled, with three good chops against the rope, I severed just enough for Bad Weather to pull the rest off of him.

As soon as he was free, he embraced me and cried, "Bless you, bless you," into my ear, until a peel of thunder brought him back to his proper senses.

Toussaint then pulled back so that his head was just a few inches ahead of mine, and said, "I need you to trust me and do what I say. We're going to save the ship."

I nodded, though the idea of doing more frightened me. "Wh-what do you need me to do?"

"We're getting the jib back up," he said, "And we're going to sail into the storm. The waves are going to keep getting bigger, and if they hit the back, the back of the boat, hold this." He shoved ropes into my hands while grabbing others from the rigging up upon the forward mast. "The back of the boat is the weakest, not made to hit waves like the front. It'll give in if it takes too much of this. Now hold steady." Bad Weather took the cutlass from me and brought it up against one of the ropes. "When I cut this, the jib is going up. I'll man it. I need you to man the wheel."

I balked. "But I don't know how to sail!"

"Turn in the direction I point," he said. "You can do it. I believe in you."

He cut the rope, the sail burst out, and the *Triton* launched forward. The small, triangular sail did not look like it was built for winds

11

this powerful, and it immediately started making noises like the crazed flapping of a giant bird hurtling down towards the sea.

"Hurry!" Bad Weather shouted over the din, his arms struggling from the effort of holding the sail in place. I had no choice. I ran to the wheel in the back. It was spinning wildly when I arrived, while the *Triton* tacked to starboard and the pirate frantically pointed his arm out in the other direction.

I may have mentioned this before, but I was not at all strong. I was always sick as a child and had never eaten enough. The wheel frightened me, spinning in its ravenous fury, but I summoned all the courage I had in my body and jammed my wrists into the whirling spokes. I cried out in pain as they crushed both my arms at once, but I stopped the spinning, and, once the feeling started to return to my hands, I grabbed ahold as I'd seen my uncle do before.

To turn the wheel at all in these conditions, I had to put all of my weight on it at once and jump onto a spoke, and sometimes immediately afterwards I would lose my grip and the wheel would spin back the other direction, losing half my progress. Bad Weather eventually gave me the signal to hold steady. He had found some good tack with the jib, and finally it was catching wind without flapping. We were at last flying smoothly forwards.

What I'm going to say next may seem unreal. Perhaps it is. I can't speak for my sanity from that night, much less for my pirate friend's. It was dark and loud, and my body from head to toe was covered in a freezing rain that no doubt could be at fault (after all, as I have said already, I am susceptible to illness). But all that being said, this is what I felt in that moment. It wasn't something that I saw or heard, but I somehow knew, really knew, that the storm was going to try to kill us.

I felt like my sense of the world around me was at once dimmed and sharpened. The sounds dulled almost to silence, and my body went numb. I then perceived with some other sense a malevolent presence coming from the storm. I followed Bad Weather's gaze out to port, to the center of the tempest. What were once lonely specters—the baleful low-hanging clouds that had wandered across the heavens through the afternoon—had now become a congregation. They spun around each other in a great ritual, whose purpose could only be to summon destruction. Bad Weather stared at that storm's center with mania in his eyes. He shouted something out into the air that looked like a taunt and laughed and yelled and laughed again. Like a madman.

I didn't know if it was invisible—I didn't even know if it was here in the physical world—but something malicious kept throwing up great pillars of foam and inky seawater against our ship. When Toussaint ran down along the railing, a glissando of foam trailed after him, as wave after wave crashed against the hull, and he called back, "Olé." The monster, spirit, devil, whatever it was that directed the storm, chased after him as ineffectually as a great beast pawing after a fly.

Then the biggest wave I'd ever seen smashed into us, swallowing up the whole prow and Bad Weather himself underwater. When the ship popped back up to the surface an eternity later, I couldn't see him.

"Bad Weather!" I screamed and abandoned the wheel, running down the stairs to the main deck.

Before I could get to the front, Bad Weather came swinging up around the side. He had a rope tied around his waist, and was laughing at the ocean with that same manic triumph for daring to think it could drown him, and I realized with a shock that he was having fun.

The wheel that I'd left behind spun until it hit its end, then the *Triton* lurched to the side. The jib caught a gust of wind and ripped straight from its anchorage, with a great tearing sound that sundered my spirit in the same instant, for it was my fault.

Then the pirate saw me wobbling between the masts and his smile died, because at the same time that he saw me, the storm monster saw me as well.

The water stopped surging. The waves around us all died down for a moment, and I felt in that sudden calm the same sense of unearthly unease that I'd felt just a moment before, when staring out into the storm's swirling depths. Then the deck suddenly dropped down from under my feet, down into a deep trench between waves, and I completely lost my balance. It left me stumbling, while Bad Weather started towards me.

"Hold on!" he yelled to me across the lull, but it was too late.

Wind and wave crashed into the ship at once, as though the entire lull was the storm drawing back its leg for a kick, and I went tumbling out over the railing. My hip clipped something as I went over and set me to spinning. Up and up I tumbled, with the darkness of the clouds and deep switching places. Even as I reached out to grab hold of something, anything, I didn't know which direction to grasp, and simply fell into the trench.

The slap of water against my arm stung it, and then I was underwater and everything was silence. With barely anything in my lungs, I flailed in the direction that I thought was up, but as the wave continued over me, I was suddenly very, very far from the surface. I floundered against it, but the turbulence of the surf pushed me back down into the depths of the monster's great black maw.

I could only drown.

I felt the arms of an angel wrap around my chest and pull me up. I thought that he must be taking me to heaven. Then we broke the surface.

"Hold on," Bad Weather shouted in my ear.

He spun me around onto his back and fastened my wrists together across his chest, clapping them to make sure they were solid. Then the rope that tethered him back to the *Triton* suddenly pulled itself taut, and we were dragged along across the surf at the same speed as the ship. He held my wrists together with one hand, while the other held onto the rope, and only once he was sure that I could keep ahold of him did he begin to bring us in.

With a methodical rhythm, he pulled us along his rope, hand over hand. Even as we were pushed underwater again and again, he kept to the same steady hand over hand. He was stronger than I'd ever imagined. I watched his arms moving in the moonlight, and could see the muscles rolling under his skin. I didn't know how he did it but, ever so slowly, Toussaint pulled us closer in.

As we drew near the *Triton*, its hull began tilting back over us, too fast, so that it looked like it would topple. Even then, Bad Weather kept up his pace, until the barnacle-encrusted wood hit us and ground us into the ocean. We were crushed between water and wood, and I very nearly lost my grip. My wrists slipped out of each hand, and I in a panic clawed at the fabric of his tunic. I accidentally dug my fingernails into his flesh instead, and the sudden pain made him cry out underwater, spewing a burst of bubbles from his mouth. Bad Weather's hand immediately went to mine and, grabbing ahold of my wrist, tore it away from his chest. He held it against his shoulder for the long while we spent underwater, until finally the boat rolled back in the other direction and we burst to the surface, both taking explosive breaths of rainy air.

The *Triton* was still rolling on the ocean, but it didn't force us underwater again. Bad Weather climbed up the hull with me on his back, until another wave hit as we just peaked our eyes up over the side—a big one that appeared over the far railing and lifted the whole ship up, before slamming it down under a second wave even bigger than the last. Almost the entire deck went underwater at once. I held onto the pirate for my life, and he held onto the rigging, and when it shot back up out of the surf a moment later, we were still alive.

We both fell, sputtering, onto the deck. We landed on our backs, side by side, with all of our energy spent. I braced myself for the storm monster's next attack, but it never came. It seemed that the beast was as spent as we were, having spent all of its best attacks trying to keep us from climbing aboard. The next wave that hit us was smaller, and the one after that smaller still. The waves were receding, and the storm's swirling center continuing on its journey off away from us. The only waves that hit us now were the desperate flailing of a monster that had already spent the bulk of its energy.

Bad Weather was smiling. He started laughing a laughter that mixed with the coughing out of sea water from his lungs. When he turned to me, his expression was pure, exultant triumph. He had eyes that I could see the demon in—eyes saturated with blood. He stared down at his own hand, with its fingers stiff from pulling us both over and over into the ship, and he clenched it into a shaking fist.

Even exhausted as he was, the pirate leapt to his feet to taunt the fleeing storm one last time.

"Is that all you have?" Bad Weather yelled. "I can continue. I can do this all night. All my cursed life long. That's right!"

It scared me to see him so animated with madness, with his wet hair loose and sparkling in the moonlight, but I also remembered how he had used that madness for my sake. He was angel and devil in one. I stared at his heaving shoulders in wonder while he watched the storm fade into the distance.

A little while later, when the rain was down to a drizzle, Bad Weather began his getaway. He jumped up into the ship's spare sailboat—a tiny little one-mast pinnace, made for quick visits to port while the *Triton* itself remained in the harbor—and quickly evaluated its condition. It wasn't strong enough for sailing across the Atlantic, but it could make it between most islands in the Caribbean, in calm waters.

"You don't mind if I take advantage of the circumstances to make my escape, do you?" he asked me, while untangling the ropes and pulleys that would lower it into the water. I was loitering around him, feeling conflicted, and not making myself at all useful. "I mean it really would sully your act of bravery if I survived the night only to be hanged on the morrow, wouldn't it?"

"But they wouldn't hang you," I objected. "If we tell them what happened, that you saved my life, they'll pardon you, won't they?"

"My lucks not that good, mademoiselle," he said with good-natured chagrin. "They'll assume this boat was lost in the storm, and me as well. So just go inside and pretend to have slept through it all and you'll be okay."

"But," I didn't know what to object to. The idea of going back inside the cabin just filled me with dread and sorrow. "Will I ever see you again?"

He laughed a mirthless laugh. "For your sake, I hope not. You barely survived one night in my company."

As Bad Weather began to lower himself down to the water, I clutched at the railing on the side, feeling desperate to stop him.

"I know," I said. "I owe you my life."

"You saved mine first."

"I don't want to go back. I want to come with you." I realized only after the words were out of my mouth that they were true.

The pirate paused in his lowering of the boat, but he wouldn't look at me. He hid his eyes under a curtain of wet hair as he said, "I can't let you do that."

"Why not?"

"My true curse," he said sadly, "Is not that I have bad luck. Not for me, anyway. I survive. Look at me now, on my own boat, sailing free, after you almost died." He wrung the rope about his hands, and still wouldn't look at me. "No, it's the people near me who suffer."

"But I've been suffering," I said. There was something happening inside me—a cracking in the rime—that I didn't understand, but I didn't want to stop. "I suffered before you got here, and I'll suffer more if I'm left alone."

"I'm sorry," he said, and he really sounded it.

I didn't have the words to describe what I was feeling, but I tried my best, stumbling forward in my desperation to keep him from lowering the boat further. "I feel like...there's something that I need to talk to you about, something you know and I don't; a lesson you could teach me about how to be free. Like you. There's something...there." I jabbed a fist against my heart. "I don't know what it is. I'm sorry, I wish I knew what I was saying..."

He remained in the same spot, bouncing against the ship's hull as it swayed in the ocean. When he answered me at last, his voice was controlled, and forced deeper than usual. "It's okay, Mademoiselle, I hear you with my heart. I understand. Your spirit and mine are the same." When he looked up at me, he smiled because it was his habit, but his eyes were wet. "But I'm too tired of people dying because of me."

I wanted to say something, give him some assurance that I wouldn't die, but I could make no such promise. I hadn't the confidence that it was true. I still thought that I was small and weak and not made to be a pirate. Still, I wanted to go.

"I don't care if I die," I said at last. "It'll be better—"

"And do you think I won't?" he interrupted. "You think I won't care when you die because of me?"

"I didn't mean that," I mumbled.

Toussaint was quiet for a long time. Then he said, "I am sorry, truly. And I do hope we meet again. On land." He gave me another sad smile. "You don't need me to take you away. You are stronger than you think you are. You can make your life worth living on your own, so don't throw it away on me."

Then he took my hand and kissed it like a gentleman.

"Adieu," he said, and lowered himself into the water.

I watched him sail away for a long time: until he was too small to make out on the horizon. The sky was starry by then, and I could see his shimmering shadow shrink against its backdrop. It wasn't going to be my last time seeing him, far from it, but at the time it felt like my entire story had come to its end. I had said to myself that I wished to have just one sip of a life that wasn't the gloomy domestic existence that had always been promised to me, and here I'd had it. The storybook of that life was now open and shut in a single night, and it was time to return to the gloom. I tried to paint it to my memory; I wanted to hold it all there, because it would need to last me the rest of my days. I wanted to remember exactly how he smelled when he held me and said bless you, bless you my angel, bless you. I wanted to remember how his arms looked while he was pulling me to safety—stronger than the whole of nature arraigned against them.

I was wrong, of course. As you should know from a glance, this is only the first chapter in a longer story. Sometimes beginnings can feel like endings, and it's not until they're done with that you can tell the one from the other. This was the beginning of my pirate legend: a small and shivering girl, mooning over a man, in sorrow. The end would be different.

Two for Mirth

I n the morning, everything seemed to return to normal. My uncle and his crew all made the same assumptions that Bad Weather had expected them to make, and none suspected a thing of me. How could they? I appeared unchanged: draped over the aft railing, with as little care to act in defiance of my uncle as I had ability to do so. I was still melancholic, though now my more general unhappiness was punctuated with memories from the previous night, which kept coming back to me as waking dreams. I would remember the feeling of his hand on mine and of his lips brushing my fingers, and, in remembering, I felt the ghosts of these sensations buzzing against my skin. I savored them.

When Port Royal came into view at last, it appeared more like a festival of boats than a town. Only the tip of the island was dock-equipped, so most visitors had to anchor out in the harbor, and the surrounding sea was choked with many more ships than could ever fit at port. As we got closer and I started to see some of the shape of the city that was to become my home, my mood soured. It looked run-down. Port Royal had recently suffered both a fire and an earthquake, and it still bore scars from these disasters when the storm hit, spewing flotsam all up and down the beach. Surly looking scavengers picked like rats through this rubble, looking for the kind of treasure that could buy them a night of pleasure in the city, which was what it was best known for (although not yet by me).

Port Royal was the seat of the Royal British Navy on this side of the Atlantic. It was also the capital of British piracy in the Caribbean. One might think that the first would preclude the second, but no, both soldiers and pirates were men of a type to spend their wealth—hard-earned or ill-gotten—on the entertainments of port. Here, there were more taverns per block than probably anywhere else in the world. Every fourth building was either a tavern or whorehouse, and men of both sides gathered in front of them to drink weak grog and prepare for the evening's festivities to begin.

We arrived just before sundown, and my uncle took me straight-away to meet my fiancé, his friend, the governor. The city was just waking up for the night, and the drinking men called out to me with whistles and the kind of rude comments that such men are liable to make. I was shocked by how forward they were in front of my uncle, whose usual aura of puritan disapproval did unusually little to sober them. If this was how they acted when I had him as a chaperone, I did not like to think what it would be like to wander these streets alone. They made suggestions the likes of which I do not wish to share with you—you can use your own imagination—but suffice it to say, they did not endear me any further to the port.

I was also feeling the effects of the heat, which was of a wet and unpleasant kind that grew more oppressive the further we went from the sea. Its grossness was made all the worse by thinking about how I'd have to live in it for years and years. My sour mood curdled so that as we neared the governor's wide, white mansion, I finally blurted out to my uncle:

"What if I don't like him? Will I still have to marry him?"

"You'll like him," my uncle grunted.

It wasn't a real answer, but it shut me up regardless. I knew that I was irritable, and I was still the type to hold my irritation inside myself rather than let it affect anyone else.

We met the man who meant to be my husband in his study, which was well-maintained and well-stocked with books. The window in the back was high and narrow, squeezed between bookshelves, and the small breadth of its sunlight made the whole room feel horizontally pinched. The overflowing shelves excited me more than the man between them, who was bent over his desk, making scratches on some document, so that the first thing I saw of him was a great, glistening bald spot. His expression was serious, focused on the work in front of him, but as soon as he looked up and recognized us, it cracked into a grin.

"There you are," he said, getting up from his chair to greet us. "I was beginning to fear that you wouldn't make it today after all. The storm and all."

"We sailed through it, sir," said my uncle.

"Did you? Of course." Governor Cormorant chuckled. "When Peterson says he'll be there on the ninth, by Jove, he'll be there on the ninth." The governor wiped his hands on his trousers. He was an English aristocrat—no more a native to this climate than I—and he was sweaty all over. "And this must be the lovely Miss Goldenleaf, is it? A genuine pleasure to meet you."

He took my hand to kiss it, as was customary for such gentlemen. It wasn't his fault that my day had been one of romantic fantasies, wherein my imagination had been caught on the memory of a beautiful man's lips on my fingers. It wasn't very fair to compare the two, but I compared them anyway. The governor was my same height, and when he took up my hand from me, it felt like he was savoring the culmination of a long period of anticipation. I felt coveted in a way that made me uncomfortable. His hand was also rather clammy.

I responded with a stiff, "Good evening, sir," and a half-hearted curtsy.

"She is exactly as you described her," Cormorant told my uncle. "It is truly love at first sight."

"As I knew it would be," Peterson said. "I appreciate you keeping a dock open for us."

"Of course," he said. "I know you, my friend. You are committed to your schedule; storm or naught."

"It was nothing but a rough night of sleep, sir. We were loaded up heavy enough to weather it, so I struck us through the night."

"My good man." Cormorant gave my uncle a hearty handshake. He seemed to hold him in very high regard.

It irritated me to hear my uncle's stubbornness made into a virtue, especially when we very well could have been lost at sea if I hadn't acted against his "schedule." To hide my frown from both men, I turned it towards my fiancé's bookshelves. The two men continued to converse about the journey and get into the gritty specifics of the shipping contract between them while I perused the collection.

My father was a bookbinder, and I had some familiarity with the craft (although it was only with great pleading on my part that I was ever allowed close enough to touch the press). I had expected for books to be my primary entertainment on this side of the world, and so I conducted my investigation of them with a seriousness that turned quickly to disappointment and then to despair.

The Jamaican governorship changed hands often—usually once every two or three years—as the position was used either as a stepping stone for those on their way to better things, or as a post of exile for those on their way to retirement. These shelves knew the changing hands of many governors, all of whom felt entitled to take back their favorite books with them when they returned to England. All that was left were dry manuals about practical things like the constructions of forts, which would be of no use to a man leaving his governorship behind. The rest were in poor condition, or related to some pocket interest so esoteric as to not warrant the cargo space needed to ferry them back to England.

While I was languishing at the idea of reading about irrigation every day, Governor Cormorant retrieved Peterson's payment from an elegant chest nestled between bookshelves. The sound of clinking silver lasted a long time—it was at least a hundred pound sterling—which he counted out in large enough quantity to fill two melon-sized satchels. He then locked the chest with a key that he kept on a cord around his neck.

"Now come along, dear," Cormorant said, sliding an arm around my waist. "There will be plenty of time for that later. Our supper awaits us."

He wasn't a particularly strong man, but he steered me around with an authority that left little room for resistance. Not that it was my custom to be resistant. But that didn't mean I liked it.

The feast that awaited our arrival in the dining room was unlike anything I'd eaten back in England. The centerpiece was a roasted pig, which tasted very salty and strangely of smoke. There were also foreign fish and weird, sweet fruits that stung my tongue. It was a celebration of the local cuisine, said my host, as well as a welcome to me. He pulled out the chair for me and piled up my plate with a sample of everything—much more than I could eat.

The governor explained to me that he was a widower, whose first wife had died soon after moving to Jamaica. He wanted me to be healthy and happy, and, if anything on the table was not to my liking, then he would send away for something I was used to. I didn't want anyone to make a hassle for me, so I pretended to like all of it, which made him very happy. He laughed at the way that I ate (so delicately, as he called it), and urged me to eat more.

Governor Cormorant called me beautiful. He thought of me as much more beautiful than I thought myself and took every opportunity to make this opinion known to me. He told me that he liked my cheeks, which had freckled terribly on the sunny journey over, and how my hair never straightened at the ends. He liked how small I was, and how my various knobby joints fit in his hands. I had a better idea now of how I came to be recommended to him as a bride: my uncle and he must have talked in one of their late-night drinking sessions about what kind of women they liked, and whatever strange preferences that my fiancé had shared with Peterson happened to align with me. Thus, my uncle brought me before him like a rare thoroughbred, a spectacular gift to be treasured without doubt.

I was treasured. I was.

Over the next few days, while the governor hosted me in the spare room that had once belonged to his wife, I tried my very best to be happy. He wasn't a wicked man—he was actually better than I had expected him to be—so I attempted to picture what my life would look like there as the governor's wife. Where would I fit in? He had servants to attend to the daily maintenance of the house. His kitchen boasted a professional chef and sous-chef to prepare his meals for him. I had never been much for cooking or cleaning myself, but I had always thought of them as skills that I ought to be improving, and would have to use one day, when I became the lady of my own house. Now, I supposed, my purpose was to bear children, though that thought filled me with dread.

My fiancé was almost always at my side. He didn't like for me to be too far away from him, so he had me read in his study while he worked, and if I were ever to leave, then he would get up and walk with me. He opened every door before me, and generally acted as though I were made of glass—liable to break with one wrong step. I'm sure that this attitude came from his last wife's death, which must have been a shock to him, and I tried to forgive it, but I did hate to be treated so.

Had we never stopped for the pirate in Antigua, I might have been wooed. I might have been flattered into contentment for long enough to marry, and maybe even longer. I would have accepted the future in this house as but a second shade of unhappiness, no worse than the first, and received my husband's effluviating affection with the same tight-lipped compliance that I'd given to the rest of the men in my life. But I had weathered a storm. Although none of them knew it (nor, probably, would believe it if they knew) I had saved the lives of my uncle and all of his men. I had swum in waters as black as the void of a starless night, and thrashed against a demon trying to pull me down under. I had more in me than this. I don't know whether this feeling was planted in me that night, or whether it had always been in me, sequestered somewhere deep in my gut, and the pirate had simply dislodged it from its hiding place, but now that it was free it would not quiet down. It rattled when my fiancé spoke of my delicate features and the weakness of my body; when he commanded me to stay at his side; when he moved me around with a hand on my back or my shoulder like I was his doll to pose. I wanted to be more than a doll. I had more in me than this.

I dragged my feet about speaking with either my fiancé or my uncle about wanting to go home. I so loathed to make people upset. Cormorant treasured me, and would, of course, be reluctant to let me go, but I was just as worried about my uncle's reaction. If he had brought me here as a gift, then how would it hurt his relationship with the governor if I asked him to take the gift back? I didn't want to be responsible for that.

When I first tried to kindly broach the topic with my uncle, I did so with many apologies, and a great deal of talking around the matter in circles, so that I don't think he knew at first what I was saying, and when he finally realized that I wanted to go back to England with him, he snorted at what he saw were the ordinary worries of a bride approaching her wedding day.

"You worry too much," he told me. "Cormorant will make a fine husband for you."

"I know, he probably would..."

"Spend more time with him. Get to know him better. You'll learn to love him," he said, and that was that.

I tried to speak with my uncle a few more times before he was scheduled to leave for England, but he was obstinately opposed to listening. On any other day about any other issue, he would get his way just by saying it would be so. I felt like I was stepping on the toes of his great plan for me, and that to push would only invite wrath, but my time was running out, and I couldn't let him get his way this once. Just this once.

On the morning when my uncle was scheduled to leave for England, I showed up on the *Triton* with my bag packed before he was even up for the morning. The deckhands were busy readying the ship to sail, and they watched me with a nervous awareness that I was not supposed to be there. None of them made to chase me off, but waited to see what my uncle would have to say about my being there.

It came as a surprise to me just how good it felt to be back on the water. I leaned over the aft railing, savoring the sea breeze while I waited for the confrontation to come to me. It cooled my nerves a bit to look over the whole golden-tinged expanse of the ocean after sunrise. The air tasted good. It felt easier to breathe up here than it had the entire week in port.

When Peterson emerged from his cabin and saw me, his first reaction was to be confused.

"Mariah?" he asked. "What are you doing here?"

"I cannot marry him, uncle," I blurted out. "I'm really, truly sorry."

"Did he...do something villainous?" Captain Peterson asked, rubbing his eyes.

"No, he," I stammered, trying to find the words to make him understand. "There's not a villainous thing about him. I only...I don't wish to be here, that's all. So will you please take me home with you?"

It was a hard sentiment for him to understand. He was a free man. He had always been the one to make the plans; he didn't know what it was like to merely go along with them. But I had hoped that he would respect me, and my father, enough to trust that I wasn't making this decision frivolously.

"'There's not a villainous thing about him'," he repeated, his words sharp. "So what is the matter?"

"I...don't want to be his wife," I said. "Not only his wife, is what I mean. I want to do something else with my life. Something more. I don't know what it is that I want to do yet, but I know that I won't be happy—"

I was cut off by my uncle's ugly, grunting laugh, which turned uglier and more scornful as it repeated itself.

"You don't know how lucky you are," he told me. The coldness of his tone made me take a step back, but he followed me. The bulk of his belly to took up the space between us and pushed me up against the rail. "I've done you a good turn here. This is a governor. You had no prospects—nothing—and I brought you a governor. But that's not enough for you? You want 'more?'" He shook his head. "You're never going to be *happy*, Mariah. Not with anyone. They're never going to be good enough. Because you're just an unhappy person; the problem is you. Nothing wrong with him, pah, I know that. He's not what's wrong." The captain jabbed a commanding finger back at the port. "So go back there and learn when something is good enough, goddammit."

"No," I said, shaking all over.

"Excuse me?"

I shoved out my chin, trying to strike a defiant pose. "I won't." My throat was wobbling too much for me to say much more. "Take me home."

"You won't? That's it? Fool girl, it's for your own good." He rubbed his eyes again, looking like I was giving him a headache, and I, fool that I was, even felt guilty for that. "And what about me, hm? You want to make a liar of me? Make me sneak you out from under his nose? With no other plan but a whim, hm?"

"Uncle," I sputtered tearfully. "You know I wouldn't do this just to hurt you. I know you don't understand, but please, just trust me—"

Peterson snorted. "*I* don't understand? I know what's good for you, girl, better than you do. So you will do as I say. You." He jabbed a finger at a nearby sailor, who was pretending not to be listening. "Carry the lady's bag down to the dock for her."

I said, "No," but I was so much smaller and quieter than him.

"Now," Peterson barked, and the sailor jumped to it. I raised a helpless hand, as if to stop him, but Peterson seized my wrist with his meaty fist. He growled at me, "Don't make me tell him to carry you down too."

I sat with my bag on the dock for a long time while the *Triton* prepared to depart. Maybe I wanted to give him a chance to come back and tell me it had been a poor joke, and apologize, and say that he loved me like a niece and of course he would take me home to my father, but he never did, and soon I watched as the ship that had brought me there shrank into the horizon. It felt like my lifeline had been severed.

A light rain began to fall. The clouds were thin, and sunlight still shone through them. Many dockhands continued to work through the gentle rainfall, loading and repairing and preparing, and I remained there with them. I kept looking out at the harbor, because there was nowhere else to go except for back to the governor's house, and to go back there felt like resigning myself to that fate.

I had never felt so alone in my life. I spent most of my time alone as a child and had not minded it then. I liked books, and I liked to daydream, and those were both solitary activities. The ache of loneliness had sometimes come to me in my solitude, but it had always been quiet. Today, it was loud. It roared in my soul. With my face frozen forwards, I felt as though stuck in a waking nightmare. I wished that Bad Weather was there to wake me up. I wished that I had gone with him. I wished that he would come to set me free.

The harbormaster came out to me after a while. He was a salt-crusted sailor, wearing a wide scrap of old sailcloth as a hood to protect his head from the rain.

"Lady," he said to me. "Lady? You need help?"

"No, thank you," I said, still staring blankly out to the sea. "Wait, sir, do you know if any of these ships are going to England?"

"Just that one that just left," he growled, then pointed to another. "The *Imperial*'ll be headed out to Watling's in the mornin'. Ye could find a way back over from there a lil easier, but ye shouldn't be traveling alone, lady. Have ye got a feller coming to take ye over?"

I shook my head. "How much would it cost me, do you think, to book passage across the ocean?"

"I'd find it hard to book fer lessen 10 pound, but really, lady, the open ocean's no place for a woman alone."

I had expected that. It was far too much to ask for as a gift from my fiancé. My father's bookshop's yearly earnings came out to about 60 pounds in a good year.

"Thank you, sir," I said, dully.

I drifted back home to my betrothed soon after, not wanting to be out in the city alone after dark. He was in a fit of worry and fawned over me as soon as I came home. He smothered the wetness from my head and shoulders with a towel and then sent for a servant to draw me up a bath. I feigned weakness to get away from him, and spent most of the day in my room, pretending to sleep.

My room was made up like a lady's; although, just like the book-shelves in the governor's study, it was furnished with an ugly amalga-mation of styles from many governors' contradicting wives. The bed was piled with many frilly pillows of different sizes, and a stack of blankets too thick to use in the heat. The wardrobe was full of old clothes—unwanted or forgotten castoffs from old governors and their wives. Many mirrors of bronze and silver, both square and round, reflected my misery back at me.

I wanted to see the rain as an omen that Bad Weather was going to come find me. While I sat in the dim light, watching droplets race down the window glass, I prayed for the window to burst open, and for the pirate to pop his pretty head through and whisk me away from this dreadful place. *Come along, mademoiselle, adventure awaits.* He never did.

He had told me that I was stronger than I thought I was. He said that I didn't need him to save me. I didn't believe him.

That evening, I sat through supper in silence while Cormorant prattled on and on about our wedding, which was approaching much too fast, and how he couldn't wait to marry me. He joked that he had half a mind to grab the minister from his dinner table and make him perform the ceremony tonight. I picked at my food, but couldn't stomach a bite of it.

I asked him, "What if...I don't think the weather is agreeing with me?"

"That, my dear, is why I must keep you inside. No more wandering in the rain." He grabbed my shoulder playfully, while I seized up beneath it like a mouse in a falcon's shadow. "You will be kept under a blanket, and I will serve you soup by the spoonful until you are feeling better."

"But would you allow me to return to England, if I asked?"

"Of course, we will return soon enough. I wouldn't ask you to bear this dreadful climate for long. I hope to have a seat in parliament waiting for me in three years at the longest."

"Must I...?" I muttered, but hesitated before finishing the question. Could I really ask him if I could be freed from our contract? "If I, if something kept us from, if I didn't want to be married...what would happen to me?"

Cormorant looked confused at the question. "Is something the matter, dear?"

"Not...the matter." My throat stuck dryly together. "I only worry that this might not be a perfect match."

He shook his head, and said, with some wry humor, more to himself than to me, "It's natural. Natural to fret, my dear, but I assure you that this will pass. Any fear, any unhappiness, will be gone once we are wed. You will come to love even this sweaty island, such that soon you will be begging me to stay rather than to go." He laughed, set back down his goblet of wine, and then grabbed me around the neck. It was so sudden, I couldn't react. I was caught in his talon, and froze within it. He didn't throttle me, didn't squeeze—he only pet the underside of my chin with his thumb, following after as it flinched away. "I will not give you up easily, my love. I am too smitten, too much caught in your spell. I am a hooked man, and you will have me soon, for better or for worse." He took a deep, rattling breath. "In sickness and in health."

His breath seemed to restore to him some manner of control over himself. With a sigh, he let me go, and soon had his talon wrapped around a glass of wine instead.

"I hope you forgive me that one bout of madness, dear," he said to me, once he'd taken a deep draught of his wine. "I feel as though you were driving me to it, testing me, weren't you? Teasing me?" He laughed again. "I assure you, I want you, and none other, for as long as I live."

I shivered as my sense returned to my body, and I recovered from the shock of his seizing upon my throat. I nodded at him, though the movement was shaky. The fluttering hope that he might help me home was cut to shreds. I did not eat another bite.

As my hopes all insisted on dying around me, I was forced to replace them with desperate plans for desperate action. I laid up in bed for a long time after dinner, conniving to myself. I made a chrysalis of my too-hot blankets and waited for the rest of the island to fall asleep. I had given providence as long as I could to send someone to help me, to save me, and I had received nothing. I didn't have a fairy godmother nor a guardian angel; I only had myself. I had to become my own hero. I had to commit an act of piracy, or else languish forever as a shell of a woman who knew that she could have been more.

I listened for the witching hour, waiting for the carousers of port to cease with their yelling, to sleep, and for the pitter patter of rain to drown out their lagging cheers. Then I emerged.

The rain muffled my footfalls as I snuck through the corridors of the governor's home, but my steps still made the floorboards creak. It wasn't an old house, but the wetness of the air made it creak like one. I did not light a candle, but walked by moonlight. My breath was shallow, and I winced at every loud step, but I kept going.

My fiancé's door was unlocked. I suppose he had no reason to lock it. The door was slightly warped, and it made a scraping sound as I pushed it inside.

In the moonlight, I could see him lying on his back in bed, with his mouth wide open, snoring loudly. He slept on top of the blanket, in a wine-stained undershirt and pants. On top of his chest sat a tarnished old key, strung up on a leather cord.

I had hoped that he would remove it before bed. I did not trust myself to pull it up over his head, so I looked around for something sharp to cut the cord with. His room came with a writing desk, and, as he was a very well-organized man, I found a letter opener exactly where I expected to. I tested its edge; it was well maintained, and quite sharp.

The snores of my would-be husband were comforting to hear in the background, as they assured me that he was still asleep; however, while I was testing the knife's edge, the sound stopped. For a moment, my heart stopped too. Then he gasped, and the snoring resumed.

As I stood over him, I had to sheathe the blade for a moment and remind myself to breathe, because I had forgotten to do so, and my hands were shaking so badly that I feared I might accidentally cut him. I was not proud to do this. He had been good to me, in a way, for the most part. I wavered. I told myself that I was stronger than I thought, and I could do this. I had to do this.

I slipped the blade under the cord in a place where it bunched and looped off of his chest. I pinned the cord to the blade with a finger on each side, then carefully sawed at the leather like it was a piece of tough steak and not a thin little thing that could usually be severed with a single slice. It took far too long, and I got a little impatient at the end, snapping the last little tendon, but he did not awaken. I slipped the key down off of the cut cord.

I fled. I did not bother to return the letter opener to its place, and neither did I close the door all the way behind me, but only shut the warped wood together as tightly as it would quietly go. It took all my restraint to keep to a walking pace as I returned to my room to breathe, breathe, and fling myself into the bed, and breathe again into the pillow.

And I was only getting started.

I delved into the closet and its repository of abandoned clothes, looking for something that I could use for a disguise. If I wanted to get off the island, it would be safer to wear trousers than a skirt, for both anonymity and safety's sake. I found much more than I needed in the closet—trousers and shirt and hat and belt and suspenders—and proceeded to experiment with outfits in front of the many strangely shaped mirrors. I bundled up my hair and tied it tight up on my head, then hid it under a stiff leather cap stained with varnish. The clothes were all a little baggy, but I did find some shirts that didn't hang too far off from my wrists, and I secured the sagging trousers with a belt over my hips. I hid the shape of my torso under layers of vest and tunic, but really there wasn't all that much there to hide in the first place.

In the mirror, I looked like an ordinary traveler—a man who was a little down on his luck, with old clothes handed down from his older brothers who were lucky enough to inherit from the family estate. I started to invent a story for myself, and it brought a smile to my lips. I just had to keep my head down, and no one would think I was the fleeing governor's fiancé. A scrappy little wharf rat, that's all they would see. I hoped.

I snuck down to the governor's study without incident, having grown braver with each journey through the halls. I stood in the doorway, squeezing the stolen key in my palm as I scanned from bookshelf to bookshelf. No one was lying there in wait. The only movement came from the shadows of raindrops in the window. The rain was dying down.

I dropped to my knees before the governor's treasure chest and fumbled the key into the lock. It turned smoothly. I hadn't gotten a good look before, when he had withdrawn my uncle's payment, at just how much money was stored there. Half of the trunk was divided into rectangular, velvet-lined pockets where pounds were kept in rows of ten coins each. The other section held loose, unsorted coins of varying origins, as well as empty pouches for parceling the treasure out. A thin, black ledger slid in snuggly between the trunk's two halves.

It was a lot of money. It was enough to pay for my uncle's entire expedition many times over. I clenched my fists on top of my knees. Even now, at the precipice, I felt bad about what I was doing—I didn't want to be a thief—but that grain of irritating sand that had stuck in me on the night of the storm had grown. One bit of dissatisfaction, for those of us who bottle it up, is nothing. Two is nothing. But when one persists and gathers more onto itself—more and more little irritants and injustices that come together and refine each other, harden each other—they turn into something else. Something beautiful. A conviction.

The misery that I would face for not breaking from him now would only fester over the years. It wasn't going to go away. Not ever. I had seen it before, in my mother, how resentment could rot love. It was she who taught me, albeit by her absence, to be unseen. I wished that my mother had run away to another life at the beginning, before withering away into a ghost in her own home. I was going to be different. I was going to be better.

I took one of the little bags and pushed open its fishlike mouth. I only took one stack of coins between my finger and thumb. The cold metal made a clicking sound as I dropped it in the bag. I left the rest of the hoard where it was.

Part of my plan was to leave a note of apology for Cormorant, to ease the pain of my departure. I flipped open the ledger to where its silk bookmark split the pages, but the content of my message eluded me. I sat at the governor's desk, jabbing his pen up and down against the bottom of its inkwell, while the rain died down to silence beyond the window. I wanted to be sincere, and I was picky about words, so I struggled for longer than I should have. Everything made me cringe at the thought of writing it down.

My uncle's name in the ledger caught my eye. It noted that part of his cargo had been lost on the way thanks to "bad weather." Toussaint would tell me more of his philosophy of piracy later, but I glimpsed a shadow of it then. It was impossible to say from the note alone whether it had been the pirate or the storm that caused the loss. Regardless of which it was, Peterson still got paid, and Cormorant got what he needed, and they both made an absurd amount of money.

I returned my gaze to the chest, and its rows upon rows of silver coins, then back to the ledger, and its rows upon rows of big numbers. Then I went and took a second stack of silver, to be safe, before leaving for the docks.

As for my note, I added it as another line in the ledger. 20 silver pounds lost to Mariah Goldenleaf. For Bad Weather.

Three for a
Funeral

I awoke to the splash of a cannonball striking the water by my head. I jolted upright, rocking my hammock back and forth. Crewmen shouted as they ran up and down the deck above me, and I heard the boom of another cannon being fired upon us.

"Hoist the white flag!" our captain bellowed. "Run it up, dammit."

I gathered my senses, remembering that I was a passenger on the *Imperial*, on my way to Watling's Island. I had been sleeping off a bout of seasickness, as a week at port had somewhat stolen my sea legs out from under me. I was curled up in the hold, hidden in a dull brown hammock. I was still dressed as a man, but did not trust my disguise to hold up as well in the light of day as it had in the darkness of early morning.

I was no longer alone in the hold. A few other civilian passengers were also making the journey to Watling's, and although it was typically more pleasant to spend the days up on deck with a cooling sea breeze about you, now all men and women who were not a part of the crew had been herded down into the hold to be out from underfoot. Nearly a dozen of us fretted together in one cramped room, full of hammocks and our luggage (the rest of the hold was dedicated to the ferrying of various commercial goods). I peered around at the other passengers over the lip of my canvas cocoon. They looked scared.

The pirate ship rammed into our broadside with a deafening crash. My hammock swung up into the wall, hitting against one of the boat's ribs, and sent me tumbling to the floor. I cried out in pain, but my cry was drowned out by the rumble of a launching invasion. Pirates bellowed out war cries as their boots hit against our deck, pistols fired their clamorous retorts, and swords sang their unsheathing songs.

It wasn't a fight. Our captain was ready to run up the flag before the fighting ever began, and the pirates' warning shots up into the sky were more than enough to cool the head of our hottest sailor. I didn't hear the clanging of metal against metal, so much as I heard the clattering of our sailors' swords hitting the deck while their hands flew up in surrender. It was over in a minute, with no casualties for either side and hardly any wounds, save for the occasional disarming slash across the arm.

In the lull after the fighting ceased, we passengers in the hold waited in silence for some order to come from the trapdoors above us.

In the corner behind the ladder, a married couple held their son between them. The little boy warbled, "Is it over?"

"Hush," a man hissed from across the room, as if the pirates would forget about the hold if we were quiet enough.

I stood up, shakily, from where the hammock had deposited me. There was an old man next to me, who I saw slipping a purse down into his trousers. "We'll be fine, son," he whispered to me. "They're scavengers. Give them what they ask for, and they won't hurt you."

The trapdoors slammed open. The pirates ignored the blocky ladder that connected us to the topside, and instead leaped straight from the deck into the middle of us. Three of them. One, a burly woman with blonde hair, cut short and feathered like a cockatoo. Another, a hirsute man, with a forest of black hair peeking out from under his vest, and an eyepatch flipped up onto his forehead. The third, a black man, with piercings in his nose, brow, and lip. The three of them bared their teeth at us, with their hands on the hilts of their cutlasses.

"What've we got here?" One-eye said as he stalked around the room, leading with a veiny, empty eye socket. It twitched with the movement of some now-defunct muscle, and we all flinched away as he drew nearer. "Hand over any coin and jewels you got on hand."

"Nothing personal," the woman said, shaking out an empty sack. "Make this easy for us, and it'll be over soon."

"*Por favor*," Piercings said, in Spanish, "[Put everything in the bag.]"

The father figure of the small, cowering family dropped off a small purse into the pirate woman's collection sack, making her grunt unhappily at him.

"You can do better than that," she said. "Look at those lovely earrings your wife has."

"Want me to cut 'em off her?" growled One-eye.

"Not yet," she said and nodded over to where their luggage was stowed behind them. "Let's open up that trunk. Find her jewelry box."

"Don't be stingy now with that coin neither." One-eye drew out a dagger, poking the little boy with the point. He sneered at the father, "Iffin you hold it back, I can tell. This eye sees all, and I'll cut out the babe's heart afore I'll let a coin go."

The man turned green. His hand shook terribly as he fished out a hidden column of silver coins from within his nicely-embroidered coat and dropped it into One-eye's sack. While the woman oversaw the dissection of their luggage, the child began to cry.

I huddled in my corner, behind the hammocks, hoping to remain unseen, but Piercings spied me. He narrowed his eyes, like he could tell that I was hiding something, then stalked in my direction. I shimmied back into my corner, but there was nowhere to hide. He ducked under the hammock, and when he straightened up, I felt like his wide shoulders were swallowing up the whole of my portal back to the rest of the world. I was alone with a dangerous man, and I wished for a weapon, or, better, a hole in the wall behind my back to fall out of and down into the sea.

Piercings made a beckoning gesture with his bag.

"Sorry," I squeaked. I took out the little fish-lipped purse that I had stolen from the governor's treasure chest, but clutched it tight with both hands. Inside was all the silver I had, and I needed it to cross the ocean.

The pirate tried to snatch the purse from out of my hands, but I yanked it back.

"I need to keep some," I said. I tried to pitch my voice lower, like a man's, but it sounded ridiculous in my own ears. When he showed no understanding, I switched to Spanish (although Spanish was my worst language). "[To go home. To England. I need it. If you take it, I will die.]"

"[This is not a negotiation]," he said in Spanish. He thumbed the top inch of his sword up out of its sheath, as an illustration of his point.

A very nice pair of boots appeared at the top of the ladder, over the pierced man's shoulder, as another pirate descended. He wore lavender stockings under black pantaloons, and a silver rapier slung from his hip. An elaborate set of overlapping tunics wrapped him tightly around his hips and shoulders. Atop his head sat a tricorne hat, underneath which a mane of black hair billowed. He smiled at us cordially.

"Bonjour," said the pirate, Bad Weather. "I apologize to you all, truly, for your misfortune. Tis not an enviable fate, not at all, to be set upon by pirates. But, alas, of the many misfortunes you might have stumbled across on these tempestuous seas, you are lucky to have come across one that will only take your coin and not your life. We only come to collect our due, we taxmen of the sea, and we will soon allow you to leave to find calmer seas and kinder tides. So, do not fret overmuch."

I stared at him senselessly. Bad Weather. Of all the ways that I had hoped to meet him again, this was not one of them.

"What do you want, Toussaint?" The blonde woman snapped up at him.

"What do I want, Ama?" Toussaint hopped down the last couple of rungs. "Why, brandy. Three dark barrels, down the port bow." At the mention of liquor, both One-eye and Piercings gave Toussaint their attention. "The captain, he has been forthright with us. So, if you big boys would do me the favor..."

Ama slapped her half-full sack into Toussaint's chest. "I'll get 'em. Zayne, with me." She snapped to the man with the piercings.

Piercings left me, blessedly, and his departure was like the end of an eclipse, when the moon departs from in front of the sun. I could see now that Bad Weather's nails were painted the blue of Caribbean waters, and that a mother-of-pearl earring hung down from one ear, shining brightly in the square of sunlight which the trapdoor let in. While the two burly pirates disappeared down the narrow passage that led to the front section of the hold, Toussaint ambled over to the small family which his crewmates had been terrorizing.

"I think she may be angry with me," Toussaint remarked to the remaining pirate, who rolled his one eye.

"Big wonder why," One-eye said, as he used a weapon that was more machete than sword to rip out the silk lining from the family's trunk.

"I have told her before that I am not the type to change."

"We'll talk about this later," One-eye hissed, and I heard in that whisper, which was lilted like a secret, a bit of the lie that he was telling us: an illusion which Toussaint threatened to dispel with every blasé breath. One-eye grunted, coughed, and returned his voice to a deeper pitch. "Go. Zayne was on the little guy."

I still clutched my tiny purse to my chest, and, as Toussaint approached me, my heart thudded so hard against it that I felt it should've made the coins jangle.

Bad Weather stopped at the old man before me, whom Zayne had mostly ignored. He whipped out his rapier, and opened up the old man's pants between the legs with one precise flick of the blade, dropping the man's sequestered coin purse to the ground.

"I would have been surprised, impressed, and sorry if that bulge was authentic, sir," Bad Weather said with a grin, as he skewered the pouch with his sword and flicked it into his collection sack.

I turned my head downward, hiding my face under the brim of my stolen leather cap as Toussaint pulled up in front of me. I hadn't yet decided whether I wanted to reveal myself. I was still a woman, traveling alone, and he was still a pirate (if a friendly one). I only saw the jut of his chin under my cap's rim, wearing a curious little half-smile, as he appeared to not quite recognize me.

"Well, bonjour, sailor," he said to me, as smarmily as if we were meeting at a tavern. "Are you by any chance traveling alone? It cannot be."

I nodded slightly without lifting my chin.

One-eye growled a warning at him from across the room, "Toussaint..."

"I am what I am," he called over his shoulder.

One-eye shook his head. "You don't have bad luck, mate. You're just a dumbass."

Toussaint shrugged like that was a good point, and when he looked back at me, he, once again, had an expression that was on the edge of recognition. "Excuse me, monsieur, but I have the strangest feeling like we've met before."

I felt pushed up to a precipice, and when I looked up to meet his eyes, I did so with a feeling like I was walking my way off of it. His eyes were the same deep, stormy blue-gray that I remembered. They widened in surprise, and even fear, as he recognized me, though he kept the smile on his lips.

"Why," he gasped, "I cannot believe my eyes, that they could be so blessed to see you again in so short a span. You...how have you come here? I..." he laughed to himself. "I daresay you've caught me off-guard."

"I left my fiancé," I blurted out, feeling that was the most important thing to say. "I'm going back to England. I...I'm amazed to see you here, too."

"It must be fate," he said. "For you to meet me once is misfortune, twice is fate. Oh Dieu," he looked around. "This is not how I wanted to meet you again."

I laughed nervously. "I thought you were proud of your piracy."

"Eh, it is ugly work," he said, kicking the floorboards. "I am ashamed at my own happiness..."

"Toussaint!" Ama snapped. She was back, with a cask of brandy atop each of her shoulders, while Zayne behind her struggled to wrap his arms around one. "This is not the time."

"It is always the time, Chéri," Toussaint said cheerily. "And might I say you look as strong as a bear; I am amazed all over again at how you carry these and yourself as well."

She sighed at him. "John…"

"Aye, I'm on it," One-eye said, going to collect from the remaining passengers in their back corner.

As Ama hoisted the first cask of brandy up to the ladder, a call came down from above. "Ship ahoy! Navy ahoy! British ship, from the west."

Ama cursed at Toussaint. "This is what you get for dragging your feet."

I was alarmed. Port Royal was to the west—had they discovered what I'd done and where I was going so quickly?—but Toussaint looked pleased at the news.

"It puts me ill at ease when things go too well," he said. "Besides, we've taken more than enough already." He gave me a wink and a furtive gesture to put my purse away. I slipped it behind my back while he blocked me from the view of the other pirates. They were distracted, rushing to hoist the brandy casks up above deck.

"Toussaint," I whispered to him. "Bad Weather. I think they're coming for me." Toussaint raised an eyebrow, and I elaborated. "I may have stolen. From the governor."

Toussaint laughed uproariously. "Did you, really?" he asked, sounding both impressed and pleased. "Why, if I ever had doubt that you and I were one in spirit…" He looked down at me with a smile that was tinged with sadness, while the pirates yelled at one another overhead about freeing their ship to set sail.

The other three pirates retreated above deck first, but Toussaint lingered. He stopped with one foot on the bottom rung of the ladder. He pulled down on the front corner of his hat, so that it hid his eyes.

"I am sorry," he said without quite looking at me. "I shouldn't have left you. I was...rattled."

I still had my silver in my hand, so I could continue my journey, if I so wished, to Watley's and then to England. The navy would give chase to the pirates, probably, and not come after me. But once I was home, I would need to rely on my father's generosity to see me to the life I wanted, and he had never shown himself to be generous with me before.

"Does that mean that...if I asked you again, your answer would be different?"

Toussaint looked pained. "You know, it is not safe to be near me."

"You could keep me safe."

"I would do the opposite," Toussaint said. "I cannot promise to keep you safe; I can only promise to value your life above my own, and that I do promise. You will certainly suffer for being near me, but if you know this and still wish to accompany me, then I will not refuse you your wish again."

My spirit swelled. To sail on a pirate ship was a very frightening thing, but my fears had always been with me, all my life. Even back in the safety of my home in England, I was afraid. My biggest fear right now wasn't anything about piracy; it was only the fear that he would take it back.

"I hear you, and I want to come anyway."

He winced a hair, but recovered enough to smile. "Very well. Then come." He continued up the ladder, and I, with effervescing fear in my belly, followed after.

Toussaint's ship—the *Villainelle*—had wedged itself deep into the side of the *Imperial*, and the pirates were prying against it with big iron levers as we came above board. The captured merchant sailors were all clustered on their knees on the foredeck, with their captain on the aft and a sword held to his throat. The surly, dark-skinned pirate who held it there was still too young to grow a beard, and only wore a thin mustache, but his blade dripped blood from where it was pressed to the captain's neck.

As Toussaint and I came topside, the prow finally groaned its last groan and came free, sawing out a divot from the *Imperial* that rained splinters into the sea. The *Villainelle*'s keel splashed back into the water, but ropes that tethered the two vessels together made it bounce back and come up alongside the *Imperial*. The pirates raised a cheer as they began pulling the lines tight to bring the *Villainelle* abreast.

"All clear below deck. All aboard the *Villainelle*," Toussaint called, and those pirates who had been watching over the crew began leaping across the gap. He cocked an immaculate black eyebrow down to me, saying, "This includes you," before taking a running leap himself.

I sucked in air through my teeth, watching the pirates leap over the gap one by one, like salmon leaping up a river. I held that sea air in my lungs as I ran after them, planted up one foot on the railing, and then flew myself across to the other ship. I landed solidly aboard, almost giddy enough to giggle.

The last pirate aboard the *Imperial* was the one who had been holding a sword to the captain's throat. The young pirate drew out a pistol to replace his sword and kept it trained on the captain until he was all the way to the railing; then, he leaped over with a whoop. Once he was aboard, we cut the lines free and pushed off.

"Hoist sail," Toussaint called out, as he pushed his way back to the helm. The *Villainelle* was configured differently from the usual British sloop; the raised captain's cabin in the aft was missing, making for a long and flat deck. I lost Toussaint in the throng of rugged sailors as they hurried to their tasks. Sailors who were already up in the rigging cut the ties from their sails to send them flapping downwards, as others

47

hurried to catch dangling ropes and pull them tight. By the time I'd woven my way through to the aft deck, Bad Weather was looking through a spyglass out towards the navy ship, which was still small on the horizon. Beside him stood a small man with bronze skin and very curly hair, who did not look at all like a captain.

"Ship of the line, third class, I'd say, 60 guns," Toussaint announced, handing the glass back. The captain said something indistinguishable, to which Toussaint boasted, "It won't even be a chase."

The wind was blowing westward, hard, back towards the navy ship. It was a beast of a boat, with multiple decks of cannons stacked up on top of each other, pointing out in every direction. They were better suited for sailing upwind than we were, so Toussaint tacked us to the northwest, just askew from charging directly towards the approaching ship. This path would take us close to the enemy at first, but with the wind in our sails, we would be able to pull away far faster than they could follow.

Our sails caught ahold of the wind with a gluttony quite unlike those of the larger merchant vessels with which I had ridden before. The *Villainelle* was a British sloop—a make of ship which was already well in contention for the fastest in the world. This particular sloop had been altered further still in the name of speed, as the pirates had taken off all the heaviest architecture that a sloop could afford to lose. The sails surged outwards with a force that felt impossible to hold as the last of our sails were secured to their proper positions. They swelled so powerfully that I feared they would explode. I kept thing again and again as we accelerated that this, this is the fastest this ship can go, and I kept being wrong.

As we closed in on the navy ship of the line, Toussaint raised the call to cut away to the north. Our trajectory would make a shape like a hook, as we tacked (ideally) just outside of their cannons' range. As we turned, the narrow deck beneath my feet began lifting out of the water on one side.

Toussaint gave the call to "Trim the Boat!" and the entire mass of pirates flung themselves over onto the rising edge of the deck, even those who were holding loose sail lines. I was pressed against the rail with them as we all collectively pushed ourselves out as far as we could go. We put every last pound that we had on our human bodies up on the scale against the wind, begging the boat to keep from tipping over. I leaned out over the side, with the exhilarating gusts pushing up against me on all sides, as I saw the ship of the line fire off its first round of cannon fire.

A big plume of smoke rose up from the multi-decked beast as several dozen cannon balls whistled through the air towards us at once. They sent up splashes as they hit the water. Perhaps we were still too far away, or perhaps they simply had not calibrated their aim to account for the sudden hook-turn, but none of the first round made contact with our ship.

"Hold steady," Toussaint called out as we continued our long arc past the ship of the line. All the crew were all still aligned on the side nearest to the cannons, using our weight to keep us from capsizing. We drew close enough that I could make out the ship's name with my naked eyes: *Weymouth*. Zayne (Piercings), behind me, chanted a Spanish prayer that they would have mercy and not shoot again.

The *Weymouth* sent up a second smoke cloud, and we all collectively flinched as a deadly barrage flew our way. The cannonballs again peppered the water between our vessels, and this time we felt the impact as one crashed into the *Villainelle* at the waterline, wedging itself into the wood. The rest landed ineffectively in the water.

Now we sped away. The *Weymouth* attempted to make chase, but it was pointed in the wrong direction, and we were soon hopelessly out of its range. Once we'd straightened out and were no longer in danger of overturning, the crew made to secure the loose sail lines, and Ama yelled out for tar to fix up the shot we took to the rear. We were almost out of eyesight before their overly-encumbered warship had turned all the way around to face us. Our crew gathered in the middle of the deck, making joyous boastings about their job well done, amidst commands shouted at them to remain alert. Still, it wasn't much longer until the other ship was lost completely over the horizon, and Toussaint gave the order to furl sail.

"Congratulations, my kings and queens of the sea," said Toussaint, wild-eyed with the euphoria of pushing our boat to the very lip of its limits. He looped steadying lines around the helm's spokes to keep it from spinning, then joined the gathering celebration, giving his crewmates firm grips on their shoulders and affectionate claps on their backs. "No casualties. No wounds. Only plunder."

When he got to me, Toussaint wrapped me up in an embrace and spun me around. It made my soul soar with the same euphoria as hanging off the boat, pushing up into the wind, sailing faster than any other ship in the world.

The crew cracked open one cask of brandy, as an immediate reward for a good day's work. The ship's cook—a long-faced woman who didn't drink and immediately retreated into the hold—brought up a big pot of turtle stew (which would have been better fresh), but the brandy on the pirates' tongues made them claim the turtle tasted like beef.

I stood nervously to the side, trying to escape notice as I sipped from a very shallow cup (shallow of my own volition). Occasionally, a sailor would give me a narrow-eyed look-over, but they were largely enthralled by their own celebration. The pirates were raucous, and I enjoyed watching them in their raucousness. Ama, although she had been abrasive earlier, loosened up with the brandy. She was a very loud drunk who loved challenging people to wrestle arms (or wrestle any way they thought they had a chance) as she growled and burped and slammed her tankard down. One-eye John had flipped his eyepatch down over his eye now (having mercy on those who needed to stomach turtle stew). He shared a tankard with a much smaller crewmate, who slipped closer as they drank more, until the second man was sitting in John's lap, with his fingers playing with the dark, curly hairs on his chest.

Toussaint and Captain Socks went over the loot together, while the latter made tallies in a notebook that looked crusty from multiple dips in the ocean. We had a good haul. The chest which they had taken from the *Imperial's* captain was full of nearly as much silver as I had found in the governor's chest, swollen as it was with our passenger fare and all that the merchants had made from selling goods in Port Royal.

When the captain and his first mate were done counting up the silver, they began passing out parcels of coin to the crew, each wrapped up in its own tidy handkerchief. This made the celebrations redouble their raucousness. Socks was offered many a grateful cup of brandy, but before he could take one and escape to the festivities, Toussaint pulled him and me aside to talk.

"Captain Socks, sir, this is Mariah. She's the one who I was telling you about, who saved my life. Mariah, this is Socrates, our captain."

"It's Tomás, but Socks is fine. There's no good in confusing people." Socks gave my hand a shake. He spoke with a very slight Portuguese accent, and had a calm demeanor about him that helped to ease some of my anxiety.

"It's a pleasure," I said, with a poor attempt at a curtsy.

"She would like to join our crew, if she may," Toussaint said.

Socks gave each of us an evaluating look. He seemed a strange type; as deliberate in his movements as Toussaint was frivolous in his. He had a reputation as a wise man, as suggested by his nickname, and an easygoing one, as suggested by its truncation. He had a very soft voice, and largely relied on his first mate to make announcements to the crew.

"I have no problem with this," Socks said at last, and Toussaint looked relieved, until the captain's expression took on a severe character. "But I'm serious this time. Follow the rules, or I'll have to let Ama give you the lashings."

"It's not going to be an issue," Toussaint said with a weak laugh, glancing in Ama's direction, where she was gloating and flexing arms over a defeated opponent.

"I hope not, you know I don't want to..."

"I know, I know, I won't."

"Aye," he turned to me. "I'll trust you to him, then. Have him show you the boat. I'm going to get myself a drink." Then he left to make good on that promise.

"Don't you intend to imbibe as well?" I asked Toussaint. "There's no need to abstain on my account."

"Alas, one man on this ship should have his mind about him, and it is best that it should be me." He smiled as if it didn't upset him at all and took me by the hand. "Come. I shall show you all our secrets."

Toussaint took me around the ship, but the tour was a brief one. Up top, the deck was long, flat, and narrow; down below, it was hollow. "Today's raid was ordinary for us," he explained as we went. "We are not ambitious, as far as pirate crews go. We go after smaller prizes; not the navy or other pirates, or anyone who looks like they might respond to us with a proper fight. We hit them hard and fast and send over our scariest men, and hope to make them surrender before they get their heads on straight. Then we take enough treasure to keep us afloat, and run away before anything can go awry."

Instead of sectioning off the *Villainelle's* inner hold into cabins, the pirates had it all gutted out. It was all one big chamber, with only the occasional supporting beam to delineate any section from the one next to it. Hammocks and cots, trunks and chests, all sprawled out seemingly at random. According to Toussaint, the space was set up this way in order to promote a democratic spirit. Their captain was there to do a job, and while it was an important job, that didn't mean that he deserved to live like royalty away from the rest of the crew. Socrates was like an arbiter; Bad Weather, a sergeant; and neither was a king.

"This can be yours," Toussaint said, showing me to an empty hammock near the foredeck. A dented cannon ball sat nearby in a splinter-sprinkled puddle, under a rushed patch job that leaked slightly. "You can keep any belongings you have down in those cubbies between the ribs on the hull, but as you saw today, we do not always stay flat on the water, so things can move, and you should keep anything you cannot bear to lose on your person for now, until you have a reputation as someone who, it would be unwise to take your things if they fall out mid-voyage."

I nodded, as the muffled shouts of a man above our heads called out, begging someone to dare him to jump off the ship (he would do it; they all knew it). I felt a little guilty about keeping Toussaint to myself, away from the festivities, but, at the same time, I felt...excited. To have him all to myself.

"And where do you sleep?" I asked, innocently enough.

He took me to his cot in the shadowed back corner, which was bolted to the floor with a velvet curtain drawn around it. His silken bedsheets were tucked around the mattress, and felt as soft as water.

He had a chest, also bolted to the floor, and a little table with a wood-paneled mirror nailed into the wall behind it.

I sat on his bed and petted his nice sheets. "As much as you have told me about your ideals of democracy, your place seems a little nicer than mine."

"Everyone has an equal share of the treasure; it is up to them what they choose to spend it on. I have been at this for nearly ten years now, since I was 16 years old, and I take my cut in nice things more than in silver. Maybe in a few years you will have the fancy bed, and I will be retired from this life."

"Is that what you want?" I asked, a little disappointed at the idea.

Toussaint gave me a conspiratorial smile. "Let me show you something." He took out a key from under his tunic and used it to open up his chest. From within, he drew out what appeared to be an ordinary fisher's tackle box. Under the lid, its painted wooden shelf was split into a dozen compartments, each of which held a different lure or hook or extra spool of line; the normal things one would find in such a box.

"You want to become a fisherman?" I asked warily.

"Ha, sneaky, isn't it?" he said, and then withdrew the top shelf from the box.

The lower shelf was overflowing with jewels. Instead of fishing tools, each of the many cubbies held its own type of jewel or precious metal. There were emeralds and rubies and opals and pearls. Pearls were the most plentiful by far, and they flowed over from one box into the others beside them like a bubbling surf.

I was awestruck at the wealth in front of me. "That is...a lot of jewels."

"If I survive this life," Toussaint said, "I think I would like to be a jeweler. I have been saving up against that future for a long while now."

He withdrew from his pocket a handkerchief, which was like those that he had been passing out to the crew, but his held jewelry instead of silver. "Maybe one day I will return to Paris, somewhere far away from where people know my name, and I will be an upstanding man." He sorted his new stones into their various sections, then replaced the false shelf on top of them. "Of course, it is an old dream," he said sadly. "The way I am now, it would all crumble to dust."

"Because of your bad luck?" I asked. "The evil spirit." He looked at me like he was surprised that I believed in it, but I had seen it in the storm; I knew it was real. I asked, "Do you know what it is?"

"I know more than nothing," he admitted. He sat down beside me but looked forward, out into space. "But it is not something that I like to talk about sober. Or at all. There are things about me that you do not know, and I'm afraid that they will change the way you look at me."

Toussaint gave me a sad smile, and his prettiness made my stomach burst into a swarm of buzzing bees. I shifted nervously, twiddled my thumbs, and looked away.

"Can it be fought?" I offered. "Maybe this evil thing can be banished. Exorcised."

"I've long given up on that."

"I'll help."

"No. It is best for you if you should keep away from me. Further than this; right now, even this is dangerous." He waved his hand across the less-than-a-foot space between us. "You poke your nose into the demon, and it will poke back, and when it pokes, people die."

I frowned, saddened. "I know I'm a coward, and there is probably nothing that I can do, but that doesn't mean that I don't want to try."

"What are you talking about?" he asked. "You think you're a coward?"

"I'm scared all the time," I admitted. "I hope that I can do something here, on this ship, with you, but to be honest, I'm a little afraid that I'm just running away."

"Chérie, you have proven yourself to be brave three times over. First, by freeing me in the storm. Second, by escaping your husband. Third, by jumping onto this ship. Three times challenged, three times proven: you are a brave woman. Understand? You think just anyone would do what you have done? No. Not at all." He took me by the arm so that I had to look at him as he spoke and see how serious he was. "You are strong, you are brave, and now that you're here, you can become even stronger and even braver. You will learn to be strong, and to keep yourself free: that's what the *Villainelle* is here for. We pirate so that we might be free, and so that we might help each other—help people like me and people like you—become who we want to be. You are just now at the beginning."

I didn't know how much I believed him. I was too cowardly to wrap my arms around him and pull him closer. That's what I wanted to do, that's who I wanted to be, right then. Instead, I nodded and wiped away at my tearful eyes, saying nothing, because to speak would be to cry, and I didn't want to prove him wrong so quickly.

"Ah, I know what you need," he said with a smile, as he shuffled himself on the bed so that he could unbuckle the sword from his belt. "This ought to be yours."

It was my uncle's cutlass; I recognized it as soon as he presented it to me. It was not pretty or shiny, like the ornamental weapons worn on the hips of people like my governor-fiancé, but it was well-made from good steel. I objected at first to his gift, out of politeness more than anything, but Toussaint pressed the scabbard into my hands until I took it.

"This is your trophy. It is proof of your bravery, though only a third of it. Whenever you feel yourself losing confidence in yourself, only feel the weight on your side, and remember that you are the reason that I am still breathing."

Toussaint smiled at me, embraced me, and whispered more kind things into my ear (although I felt less like a strong and brave pirate the more that he was kind to me). I was still unkind to myself, because before I had met Bad Weather, no one in my life had said such things to me. Now, for the first time, I felt myself beginning to believe them, and with that belief came the conviction that I wanted to become that person who Toussaint said I was. I wanted to become brave and strong and free like him. Then, I thought, I might be brave enough to kiss him, and maybe even good enough for him to kiss me back.

"If any of what you think of me is true," I said, finally, into his shoulder. "Then I will save you, Bad Weather. I will find a way to break your curse."

He looked sadly at me, brushed some of my loose hair behind my ear, and said, "It is a good dream."

I wanted to return to our embrace, but he put a hand on my shoulder and gently used it to keep the distance between us as he stood back up. "We should return to the party," he said, and offered me a hand. "Before the captain thinks I'm breaking his rules."

He helped me to my feet, like a gentleman, but kept his distance while we went back topside. It was going to be a long journey.

Four for a Birth

Before I could become a pirate, I first had to become a sailor, and I set myself to that task with avarice. I didn't want to be just some girl on a pirate ship, here for a lark; I wanted to be a pirate; I wanted to be useful and was in a rush to become so. I wanted to sail, to man the rigging, to fight—all of it, all at once. I kept dressing with the practicality of a man, with trousers and shirts that soon collected stains and tears as I worked in them. There was so much to learn, and my eyes were bigger than my hands and my arms and my legs, all of which began to ache quite terribly with the climbing and the swabbing and the tying and untying and retying.

My enthusiasm was both indulged and tested by the second mate, Ama. She was the *Villainelle's* taskmaster, and idleness was her enemy. Any ship on the ocean is always trying to fall apart on itself, and it's only by the maintenance of its crew—and the vigilant eye of one such as Ama—that it can remain afloat. The brawny blonde woman always seemed to appear over my shoulder right at the moment that I finished with a task, ready to hand me a new one. From swabbing the deck before breakfast to standing a mid-night watch, my day was full of work. I was grateful for it, even if it left me feeling as sore as if the ship itself were running me down and crushing me and rolling me out like dough.

I came to learn that, of all the kinds of places in the world, the open ocean is among the least hospitable to humankind. We are not meant to be on it. It has very little to offer that can sustain life, and the endless expanse of poisonous water—let alone that it will kill one for drinking it—constantly puts itself at war against whatever man-made thing is put out upon it. The ocean wants to reconquer the tiny sliver of space which one hull can carve out, and will send ten thousand incursions in order to reclaim that domain. It wears down the hull by those ten-thousand tiny attacks, with ten-thousand tiny holes which, were they permitted coexistence, would turn wood and tar to sponge and sink us to the bottom of the sea.

Not only that, but the constant rocking and twisting imposed by the waves upon our ship (which was, when you think about it, little more than a jiggling jumble of pieces—planks and ropes and the tiniest of nails holding them together) would continually force one piece or another from its proper position. The lines would go slack, one by one, with as much reason as magic, and we had to untie the seizing lines, pull them taut, and retie them, and always by the time one line was fixed another one somewhere else had gone slack instead. If all these myriad imperfections were left to persist and multiply, the many boards would be worked apart from one another and all fall to shambles and sink us, again, to the bottom of the sea.

So I was happy to do my part at forestalling our watery grave; that being said, it did wear me down. Ama so hated to see idleness that most of the crew hid theirs from her, and because I did not (as I wanted to be honest and useful) she saw to it that I always had more to do. My hands were worked raw by the tugging of ropes, so that they were red and marked with many shallow craters where once was skin or blister. My fingers lost the strength necessary to grip, and I'd have to loop my arms under or around whatever I needed to carry rather than relying on my hands to hold it. I was weak, and too ashamed of that weakness to show it. I simply said, yes ma'am, and scurried over to wherever Ama pointed.

"Ama, you're working her to death," Toussaint complained when he saw my hands. He held them in a tender way that made my heart flutter. The pirate would sometimes come to give me pointers and kind words of support, but I tried to look my strongest when he was near, so it took him a few days before he saw the state I was in.

"I know what I'm doing, *Bad Wezzer*," Ama said, mocking his name and accent. "You keep to your job; I'll keep to mine."

"She never has worked the rigging before in her life; you do not need to be working her so hard as you would a seasoned sailor from the very beginning."

"Mariah," she asked without breaking eye contact with Toussaint. "Would you like me to make allowances for you on this man's behalf?"

"No ma'am," I said, and meant it.

"There you go."

Toussaint would occasionally sneak by to relieve me of my work, even though, as first mate, he was supposed to be exempt from jobs like scrubbing the deck and dipping his hands in the tar. I was too tired to argue with him, but I winced at the judgment of the other deckhands doing the same job. In particular, Jaks—the serious-looking young man who had held the captain of the *Imperial* at sword-point—always gave a glower to see me so aided. It was never long before the ever-vigilant Ama would chase Toussaint off, yelling at him for coddling me, and then I was back to work after not long enough of a break at all.

I didn't realize it at the time, but for my first few weeks, I was worked the hardest of anyone aboard the *Villainelle*. On a merchant vessel, sailors were always hard at work, but this was because merchants (in their constant quest to maximize profit) hired only so many men as were absolutely necessary to keep the boat from falling apart. A pirate ship, on the other hand, scaled its profit with strength, and a large pirate crew was much more intimidating than a small one. Thus, we had twice as many people to do the same amount of work. As I worked myself as hard as I'd seen the sailors worked on the *Triton* and the *Imperial*, many of the raiding pirates spent their time hiding in crannies below deck, playing cards and avoiding Ama's tasks.

Eventually, my body collapsed on me. My head was spinning, and I could barely keep my eyes open, so I retreated from the sun down below deck and fell into my hammock to rest; however, I wasn't there for long at all before Ama came and jabbed me awake through the fabric with the wooden handle of a chisel.

"Mouse," she called me. "Come. I need someone to scrape the rust from the anchor chain."

"Yes ma'am," I mumbled, but when I tried to stand, my eyes filled with gray noise, and I stumbled into her. "Sorry, sorry."

"Steady there," Ama said, catching me around the belly. She put a hand to my forehead, didn't like what she felt, and pushed me back into my hammock.

Ama made me stay inside and rest for the remainder of the day. She never said that she was sorry—that wasn't the kind of thing she did—but she acted like she was, checking in every so often to make sure that I was still alive. She brought me fresh water and made me drink it in small sips, as well as salted beef and hard crackers. I apologized, and she called me foolish for it.

"Break the girl to make the woman," she said. "Struggle makes strength. You will know this later."

On the morrow, when I was feeling a little better, I asked her for work. She gave it to me with a little reluctance, but as I continued coming back for more, the reluctance waned, replaced by a stoic kind of approval.

After that, Ama took me somewhat under her wing. She was the busiest person on the boat, but she took time for me. She stopped by whenever I took my meals, bringing me more to eat than I wanted. She said that strength came from food, and I needed to keep eating if I wanted to become as strong as her one day (which I indeed wanted very much). She taught me certain exercises which would strengthen my arms and legs and back, in various ways beyond what work alone could accomplish. She gifted me a set of her old weighted bars, which were now too light for her, and demonstrated exercises for the stressing and growth of muscles. I appreciated all of this very much, even as it made me sore in entirely new ways.

"You're getting stronger already," she told me as I lay on my back after trying to emulate her exercises, breathing as hard as a bellows. "We'll make a pirate of you yet."

Gasping, I disagreed, "I still feel like I'm made of sticks."

"I was much the same, at first," Ama explained. "Toussaint and I both looked just as like a little mouse as you when we were new to this life."

I smiled to be reminded of him. "He told me that we were one in spirit, but I don't know if I can believe that either of you ever looked like me."

"Aye," Ama said, with an odd hesitance. "You do know how he...used to be, don't you?"

"Not at all," I said, and propped myself up to better give her my attention. "Do you know? Can you tell me?"

"You've never...?" Ama jutted her blocky chin to the side, frowning like she just spilled a secret. "Well, it's not my place to say."

"What is it?" I asked too excitedly.

"Only...don't expect too much of him," she said. "He won't change." And no matter how much I bore into her, she would not reveal more. Instead, she made me go back to work.

Things settled into a routine aboard the ship (as strange as it might seem as a place for routine). That is, until the day of the first storm.

The ship was already abustle when I arose that morning. People were busy collecting up the miscellaneous junk that usually covered the upper deck and taking it below. They tied it up in big parcels, with many coils of ropes slung around them. People would stuff more and more underneath the ropes, in unorganized consolidation, until they could not shift them at all from the parcels, and then they would tie another rope. It was disconcerting to see so many people so hard at work at once.

As I arrived topside, they were taking down the sails. The sailors did not stow them up on the crossbar, where they could simply be unrolled and restrung, but instead they untied every line completely so that the canvas could be brought down from the mast. They then folded the canvas up with four people to a sail before carrying them down to the storage below deck.

"What's going on?" I asked One-eye John, as he attempted to work apart a tough knot nearby.

"Storm's coming," he said. The sky was blue, but when he caught me looking up at it, John spat. "Don't matter what the sky look like. If Bad Weather says it's coming, it's coming."

Toussaint was arguing with Socrates at the bow, looking much more upset than the calm-mannered captain about whatever they were discussing. I wanted to come closer to listen, but vigilant Ama, master of tasks, caught me on my way and set me to help hoist the storm sails.

Storm sails were smaller and firmer than good-weather sails, made with durability in mind rather than speed. They looked somewhat too small for the rigging, so that they hovered away from the wood by several extra inches. They struck me as funny—as though the ship were wearing a set of shirts that was several sizes too small for it. We secured them with many redundant lines, in order to both reduce the strain on each individual line and to allow for a few to come undone in turbulent weather without compromising the entire sail.

We just finished securing the last of the excessive lines when the captain called for a meeting on deck. Toussaint and Socrates had failed to come to an agreement on their own, and so needed to request a vote from the rest of us. We arranged ourselves into a loose audience around the mainmast, leaving plenty of room for the two men to make their appeals in the middle. I made myself unobtrusive towards the back, while Captain Socks entered the ring to address us.

"This morning on watch, Riley spied a Spanish ship." Socks pointed out towards the sea at what could possibly be a ship, but, without a spyglass, only looked like the tiniest speck against the horizon. "It appears to be a galleon, a big one but an old one, riding low in the water. It's too large for us to consider on normal circumstances, but we have a storm coming; of which they seem to have no knowledge, or, at the least, for which they appear to be taking no action, neither of preparation nor evasion.

"We have two courses before us. The first is to follow them at a distance until the storm hits. We are trained for storm sailing and prepared for it, while they are not. We wait for the storm to sink them, mark which island they wash up upon, and return to scavenge through the wreckage once the storm has passed; or, if they are somehow still floating, we ambush them while their powder is soggy. Either way, we stand to make a great deal of money."

"We do not know this," Toussaint interrupted. "There might be no silver nor gold aboard. The galleon could be carrying anything."

"Right, it could be carrying *anything*," Socks repeated seductively. "It's the same make as a Spanish treasure ship. It could be a lagging member of the treasure fleet, separated from the main body by some chance, and full to the rafters with silver. We stand to make a fortune, with only minor risk to us, and I say that we would be fools to pass up the opportunity."

The crew murmured about this news with obvious excitement while Socrates retreated from the center of our makeshift amphitheater. Toussaint rubbed his temples as he walked up to take Sock's place. His expression was serious, and he gave us neither a smile nor a joke to open. He wore the same look of pain as he did whenever I tried to poke at his past.

"I do not want to do this," Toussaint said bluntly. "Any of it. I want to warn the Spanish ship of the impending storm, if you'll allow it."

Some of the crew reacted with surprise, but a couple of his crewmates—Ama and John among them—groaned in recognition. They already understood enough of Toussaint to know why this was his stance, and to disagree with it.

"Why should we?" Jaks asked, his combative voice cutting through the groans and murmurs.

Toussaint held his hands out over the grumbling audience, half in benediction and half in beggary. "I understand that this is not the piratical thing to do, but it is the human thing. If you see a stranger about to fall into a well, there is no sense in asking of you why should you call out to warn him? It is normal and natural to want to help."

His declaration initiated a rumble of chatter among the assembled crew:

"We're opportunists, mate. That's our creed."

"We don't owe those Spanish bastards one shit."

"It's not your fault, mate," John called, with his arms crossed. "Storms happen. It's nature."

"You cannot know that, John," Toussaint answered gravely.

Socks held up a hand, and the chatter, which was just in the process of redoubling, died down. The crew gave him their attention when he spoke.

"Toussaint is free to believe that he is the cause of every storm in the Caribbean. He feels driven by his guilt to sail up to them and be shot at and shout out a warning they won't believe. He can believe that is right, but it is up to the crew to choose our action. Let us ask ourselves: who believes that we should go and warn them of the storm? Say aye."

I gave my 'aye,' to support Toussaint, who gave me a grateful answering look. Only one other voice answered the call: Riley, a long-haired young deckhand. He raised up half of one hand with his vote, and his voice was quiet. No one else gave the captain their aye.

As I stood there with my hand raised, I heard a snort, and my eyes flickered to follow it. Jaks was giving me the most contemptuous sneer, having obviously thought that I was only giving the first mate my vote because I liked him, and I couldn't say he was wrong to think so. I jerked my hand back down in several successive, self-conscious stages, as Socks called for the next vote.

"And who thinks we should wait for the storm to come? Say aye."

The chorus of ayes that followed did not sound particularly enthusiastic; they were more of a foregone conclusion.

"The ayes have it."

The storm came on towards the late afternoon as a curtain of twisting clouds, with a shimmering shadow of ran beneath. It chased us like a creature from the underworld, soon to overtake our tiny vessel and swallow us up.

I jittered, excited to see how this storm would differ from the last one, now that I had at least an amateur's understanding now of how the sails functioned. I hoped to be useful this time, and to reap from that usefulness some sense of empowerment; however, as the deadly curtain grew nearer, I had no instruction, no sense that there was something for me to do. I thought to approach Toussaint, but he was grim about the mouth, with eyes busy searching for something in the clouds so that he didn't see me beside him. So I came up to Ama instead.

"You get below, Mouse," she told me. "It'll be a bad one."

"But why me?" I asked, disappointed. "You said..."

"There's too much you need to know that you don't. I'll show you for next time," Ama said. "Now get below."

I grumpily followed the bulk of the crew down below deck. The hold was bustling with people already, and it repaired my pride to see Socks, Zayne, Jaks, and other veterans hunkering down to wait out the storm inside.

Jaks shoved a bucket into my hands as I passed him by, growling that he didn't want my vomit all over the floor. He left me behind before I could respond with thanks or an insult, as I hadn't quite decided which I wanted to give him. I sulked in my corner of the hold, waiting for the storm to come.

It was worse than the last one. The *Villainelle* was light, and it buoyed with every surge and break of waves. We all were blind below deck to when the next rise or fall would come, so that they would continuously catch us by surprise and make our stomachs fall. At first, one lantern hung up in the middle of the room, shaking all over the place and throwing manic shadows up against every surface, but once it spilled half its oil on the floor, everyone thought it best that it should be put out. Thus, we spent most of the night in darkness.

I didn't vomit, though I spent half the night curled up with the bucket between my knees. Breakfast, lunch, and dinner all day had been hard tack—crackers baked four times over so that they're harder than your teeth—in preparation for the storm. You had to soak them in grog before they became edible, and, even then, "edible" was an overstatement. They agreed with the gut, however, even if they didn't with the palate. I longed to be up on deck, where I could see how we carved our path between waves. I would trade this nausea for that terror any day. It was a horrible, exhausting night, and I resolved to never wait out such a storm inside again.

The next morning, no one looked well-rested, but none looked worse than the storm crew: Toussaint, Ama, Riley, Gopher, and Stache. They came down in salt-crusted clothes, wet from head to toe, with shadowed eyes and haggard, haunted expressions. Everyone downstairs gave them a wide berth while they stumbled to their various resting places.

The Spanish ship was very easy to find; we only had to spot the smoke signal raised by the marooned remnants of the Spanish crew. We found their ship in the middle of a great reef, between two sandy islands which were too small for any map. It was shoved up on its side amongst several sharp, rocky pillars, cracked open like an egg, after having been dragged along the reef for a mile, leaving a trail of giant splinters that stuck out from the surf. Along the prow, the embossed name of the ship read *Buenaventura*: 'good fortune.'

"Should we grab the maroons?" John asked to the awake half of the crew as we neared the reef.

Zayne snorted. "They're Spaniards. Let 'em ask fuckin' catholic Jesus for a hand up."

"We can give it a vote after we look through their ship," Socks answered.

The *Villainelle* dropped anchor on the outer edge of the reef, so that we wouldn't go aground ourselves, and then we started making preparations for an approach. We were to go in the small, one-masted pinnace, which I suspected was the same one Toussaint had stolen from my uncle's ship. Socks asked the assembled party for volunteers.

"I'll go," I spoke up first, perhaps too eagerly, as Jaks gave me another one of his glares.

"*I'll* go," Jaks said. "You don't know what could be there. Might be survivors."

"Right, I'll be in," Zayne said.

"Anyway, do you think Bad Weather wants you going anywhere dangerous?" Jaks asked pointedly.

I bristled. "Why wouldn't he, and why would it matter?"

Jaks curled his lip. "It ain't party time out here."

"Settle down," Socks warned. "Jaks, Zayne, Mariah. You three go see what we've got."

I gave Jaks a gloating look (and immediately regretted it) as we both stepped into the same boat.

Zayne manned the sail and rudder while Jaks and I used the oars to maneuver ourselves through the reef to the *Buenaventura*. The water was murky from the storm, but even with silt swirling through the corals, the underwater world looked strange and bright and beautiful. We veered off towards the occasional floating piece of debris as we went, but whenever we pulled in a barrel and cracked it open, it only had sea-spoiled supplies, and nothing worth keeping.

The ship was broken more or less in half, with the front propped up against the rocks, while the back was stuck, half-submerged, in a trench off the reef. We drew up against its barnacle-encrusted hull, and as we neared the big hole in its center, I saw that it hadn't really been cracked open at all. The hull was pulled apart, rather than snapped; the whitish wood fibers looked much more like the tendons of a great muscle that were stretched past their limits by two giant fists than it did a broken eggshell.

Jaks tied us off to a rock, and then the three of us leaped up into the jagged hollow. The hole continued up through the decks, so that we could see a cross-section of the ship from keel to mast. It was dark inside, with the water in the submerged half looking ominous and oily.

"Either of you want to swim?" Zayne asked.

"We should go through the top half first," Jaks said.

Zayne agreed, but as we poked through the rooms, we found very little of value. The supplies were in better condition than those that we had found floating in the reef (we set aside a crate of barrel staves to take back with us) but the loot was a far cry away from the Spanish silver that we'd been hopeful of.

The hull wall was not made to be walked upon, and as Zayne climbed up towards the very front of the boat, the wood began to creak and shift under his feet. He made a hasty retreat back down before the whole vessel could fall forward.

"Mouse, you're small," he called to me. "Go poke your nose in that forecabin there."

I frowned, not liking that "Mouse" was catching on, but I went anyway. The cabin was in the very front point of the *Buenaventura*, and the walls came together closely on either side of the door, so that it didn't look like there was going to be much open space at all inside. It wasn't very hard to climb up the wall, but the wood had swollen into the doorframe, and it took me hanging all of my weight off of the doorhandle to force it open. Once the door came falling open on me, so did a man.

He was cold and wet, and he fell into my arms as limp as a fish. I screamed and dropped him, so that he went flopping down the wall. He rolled a bit and stopped by Zayne's feet, leaving a trail of blood behind him. I stared at him, amazed at his stillness, and expecting at any moment for him to break from it. His eyes stared up at me; one was yellowed, and the other marbled pink and red under a bloody film.

"What the hell?" Jaks called, poking his head out from another cabin. When he saw the body, he gave a grimace, then a dark chuckle. "Never seen a dead man before, Mouse? Did he give you a fright?"

"I'm fine," I said. "It's fine." I clutched the doorframe with white knuckles, while my other hand clutched my chest.

"Then get in there," Jaks ordered before returning to his own search.

The forecabin was in a great state of dishevelment. Cot and drawers and desk balanced heavily atop one another, with their contents strewn everywhere, and all covered in blood and ink from broken bottles. I poked through carefully, not wanting to serve myself a blunt death like that which had befallen the sailor that lived here. There wasn't much of value, but I did find, hidden in the desk's bottommost drawer, a small lockbox and logbook. Both were only slightly ink-marred.

I handed off the lockbox for Zayne to crack open with his pry bar, while I took a look at the logbook. I flipped through to the back, where the captain, whom I now surmised lie between Zayne and myself, wrote about this voyage.

"They were on their way to Spain," I informed Zayne. "Chartered under the Holy Office of the Inquisition to deliver tobacco, sugar, coffee. But also, words I don't recognize. Art objects, I think. An 'urna,' is that an urn?"

"Aye," Zayne grunted, as he finally managed to pop open the lockbox. Inside sat a tidy collection of Spanish silver, as well as several strange looking pendants and medallions of polished green stone and gold. Zayne held one of the gold ones up to the light, where it shone through broken boards, and marveled, "Diablo..."

I took one of the jade medallions, which had its own leather cord. It had the strangely realistic carving in it of a woman's face with big eyes. I polished away some of the tarnish from her hair with my thumb, then put the whole thing in my pocket.

Zayne called for Jaks to return to us, and we all gathered the middle of the boat, where the light was brightest. Jaks hadn't found anything like what the journal described either. We'd already looked through all the rooms in the front half of the ship, which left...

"There ought to be more artifacts, somewhere down there," I said, gesturing down towards the dark water and the submerged half of the boat. "Sugar and coffee may already be ruined by the seawater, but these art objects should have survived, and they might be made of gold or gemstone."

We all looked down at the oily water which filled the back half of the galleon. It looked like a different substance from the sea that lay just outside, with a slight iridescent sheen to its surface. It was darker and more sinister than reef water, with blood smeared around the edges. The surface was eerily stagnant and cluttered with floating shards of wood. Underneath, it quickly became too dark to see anything.

"Want to draw lots?" asked Zayne.

"You and me?" Jaks asked him. "I don't know. There's blood in that water; could be sharks."

"Could drown."

I volunteered, quietly, to go, but, if they heard me, neither man took me seriously enough to answer.

"Do you think we could break in through these walls?" Jaks asked, patting the cracked wall to a cabin whose entrance was submerged.

Zayne shrugged. "If we had an axe, maybe we could get through. Not sure how stable this ship is, though, we might collapse it."

"Better than swimming."

I took a step into the water. It was cold, and the floor was slippery. I took another step, and a third. Before the other two noticed, I was already up to my knees.

"Woah, woah," Jaks said, rearing up at the waterline. He reached out for me, but I took a big step inside to get out of his reach.

"I'll be right back," I said.

"Stop, now," Jaks commanded, then took a reluctant step inside. "I'm not going to be the one to tell Bad Weather another one of his girls drowned."

"I am *not* his girl."

Jaks took another step and swung out to catch me, but I ducked down backwards, into the water, and swam away.

It was dark underwater, but I knew where the first cabin door would be. I traveled along the wall by feel until I reached the open hole where the door had been before it was torn off of one hinge. I dove inside and immediately hit my head on a box that was floating amidst a great forest of crates that hung suspended in the water. Sharp wooden corners were everywhere around me. I knew that there would be air near the top, because the room wasn't fully submerged, but I had not known how difficult it would be to get there. The boxes were already shoving against each other in their attempt to reach the surface, leaving very little room for me to wiggle up in between them.

With my cheeks puffed out, and my lungs burning, I took advantage of my slenderness and made like an eel, just barely slipping through the tiny gaps. Nail heads and iron-tipped corners tugged against my clothes and my skin, opening up wounds in each, but I continued on despite their stings. Then, finally, I broke the surface with a big gasp.

Jaks hadn't followed me. He'd waited for me to come back and resurface, but I hadn't done so as he'd expected.

"You okay in there?" Zayne asked, his voice muffled through the wood.

"I'm fine," I called back.

"Then get the hell out here," Jaks shouted.

I ignored that instruction. Instead, I wedged myself up on top of a crate and pushed it down with both legs. It took some failing first, and every time I resurfaced, I did so amongst more calls from the two pirates, but eventually I managed to wedge a crate up under the doorframe. Then, with a few quick kicks, I sent the whole box floating out into the main hall.

I surfaced again inside the drowned room, but the men had not ceased their yelling at me to come back out from the water.

"Are you not men?" I asked them in-between gasps for air. "Quit fretting like grandmothers and open that crate." Then I dove back below for another one. And another after that. When I surfaced the third time, I heard them shuffling through the crate's contents.

"Well?" I asked. "What's in there?"

"Weird shit," Zayne answered. "Keep sending them out."

I did so. All told, there were about a half-dozen big crates in that room, and I didn't return to the others until I had sent back all of them. When I emerged back in the main room, dripping and cold, I put my hands on my hips, and said with a grin, "What've we got?"

Zayne stalked up to me. He took me under my shoulders, to my surprise, and lifted me out of the water like I was as light as a straw doll. Once he'd set me down onto dry deck, he took one of his big hands and stuck it right on my head, to ruffle my wet hair.

"You're mad, Mouse," he said affectionately.

"I'm not a mouse," I said, and pushed his hand off. I glared at Jaks, who glared right back. "My name is Mariah."

Jaks' bruised pride was as plain to see as a black eye would be. He chewed on his tongue while he came up to me.

"You can't do that," he spat.

"Seems to have worked out fine," I said, shrugging and looking away.

"If you don't take this shit seriously, if you do whatever the fuck you fancy, you're going to die, if I don't kill you my fucking self."

"Woah there, Jaks," Zayne said, catching him on the sternum and holding him back from me. "You know the code."

"I'm not gonna kill 'er, mate. She'll do that to herself, don't need my help." Then he jabbed his finger at me, "But if you don't show me some fucking respect, I'll beat it out of you. That's a promise, mate."

I knew for certain that he could beat me—and kill me—if he wanted to. If the two of us were to fight, he would make good on his promise, but I wasn't scared of him. I had already made the choice before not to let someone else tell me what I was and was not capable of. There was no point in making a different choice now, for a different man. That being said, I didn't want to fight him. I was silent for a long time, enough for Jaks to take my silence for compliance, and for him to grumble off in the other direction.

Then I muttered, "You respect me, and I'll respect you."

Jaks froze up, tense and silent, like he was having trouble believing what he just heard. Then he came storming back towards me. Zayne caught him again with a restraining hand.

"Take a breath, Jaks," Zayne said, low into his ear. "Cool down."

"She—" Jaks couldn't find the words, just jabbed his finger in the air.

"Take a breath, mate."

Jaks bit his tongue again, rolling his lips over each other as they chewed on his anger. "Fine," he said, and whirled around again. He stomped all the way to the hole through which we had entered before yelling back at me. "Next time we make landfall, I'm beating the lesson into you, Toussaint's girl or not." Then he jumped out onto the rocky ledge below.

Zayne and I worked unhappily together to load the crates into the pinnace. We settled into a quiet rhythm. I'm not sure that we said more than ten words together, the three of us, until we had packed up everything and made the entire journey back to the *Villainelle*.

We worked together to lift the crates up aboard, hoisting them one after another up the side, and by the time I was aboard myself, people were tearing into them.

I looked around sheepishly for Bad Weather. I worried that he would reprimand me or that he'd treat me like how Jaks had said he would: like a glass girl, like my fiancé had. But when I saw him, he smiled at me.

"Zayne tells me we have you to thank for all of this," he said, pulling out a jade-plated statuette from the crate before him. "I don't know if there's much money in these if we were to take them to sell in Port Royale, but at the very least, there should be one person who values them and will pay to have them back." He set the statuette down beside his crate, then went back to sifting through the damp straw packing.

I shuffled my feet. "Did he tell you about...how I got them?"

Toussaint laughed. "Why say it like that? He called you the mad mouse for diving in there. I told him that's just who you are. But I do see how madness and courage can appear alike."

"Oh, well, yes," I blushed and blustered. "It, that part, went well."

I started to tell him more of the trip, but recognized before too long that he was not paying attention to me. He was staring down at his hands instead, which were frozen around a curiosity from the box.

He held a mask in his hand. It was ceramic, with the brown of the old, cracked clay showing through faded and chipped green paint. The mouth was full of protruding needles of tarnished bronze, which took the place of teeth or fangs. Half of these needles were missing or bent, leaving holes in the ceramic that would have held them. It wore a crown of tombstones, and its eyes were ringed with snake-thick circle-glasses. Toussaint's eyes were as round as the mask's, as he stared at it like a man in a trance. His hands shook.

"What is that?" I asked, with a gentle touch on his shoulder that made him flinch.

"Nothing," he said, and pulled down on the front of his cap so that it would shroud his wide eyes from me. "It's nothing."

Then he snapped the mask in two and threw both halves into the ocean.

Five for Honor

The marooned Spanish sailors had been ground down quite thoroughly by the storm. They had in their possession not a single surviving coat nor hat among them, and the little clothing that they had managed to keep ahold of was all torn and stiff from drying in the sun. They were a soggy-hearted lot, and quick to relinquish their armaments and what little else they had saved from the *Buenaventura* in exchange for safe haven and passage back to Vera Cruz. We asked if, once we had ferried them back home, they could introduce us to the office of the inquisition which had chartered them, and perhaps broker a deal between us for the salvaged goods; it was a request to which they had no choice but to accede, for what did they have to barter with? The storm had broken their spirits for us, and now all that they could do was forlornly bare the company of pirates, and accept whatever quarter we deigned to give them.

The exception to this rule was an assistant clerk of the Inquisition—a Signor Ruiz—whose responsibility it had been, along with his late master, to care for the artifacts on their passage across the sea. He was a small, balding man with reddish-brown skin, whose spectacles had not survived the storm, and without them he was as blind as a bat. The small man was saddened by the fate of his treasures. He would pick through our crates, squinting down at the artifacts that he held a mere inch from his nose, and lament every scratch, dent, or missing piece.

"There was more," he whined in thickly accented English. "Many more must be there." But we were not a cargo ship, and we were not going to trawl the reef for every lost crate, no matter how much he begged us.

"Cheer up, you've earned an unexpected promotion." Zayne said with a heavy clap on the former assistant's back.

Zayne never bothered to hide how he took pleasure in being cruel to Spaniards. He was born a slave on a Spanish plantation, escaped by some resourceful trickery, and now firmly believed that the lot of the Spanish colonizers were all devils wearing the skin of men (a theory which, to be fair, had a lot of supporting evidence). He got Ruiz to quiet down about leaving the shipwreck behind by threatening to toss him out into the sea so that he could go looking for himself.

We sailed westward. It would be two weeks before we'd make landfall in Vera Cruz, so I had two weeks to prepare for the altercation with Jaks. Thoughts of artifacts and strange masks, thrown into the ocean, receded before the more immediate and bodily threat. If Jaks had expected for me to blithely accept his beating as he dealt it out, then he was going to be mistaken.

When I asked Ama to teach me how to defend myself, she didn't pry into my motivations. Before she had been press ganged into a voyage across the Atlantic, Ama had spent her childhood on the most lowdown of all the miserable streets in Liverpool, and the concept of defending oneself was, to her, no more than a natural and necessary part of being out on one's own. She was, if anything, pleased that I had come to her.

"You made the right goddamn choice," she told me. "Didn't ask Toussaint first, right? He doesn't know shit about fighting with his bare hands. Right, right, this is good." She scratched at her chin under a growing grin. "Come, to the foredeck, tis an open enough space."

"Right this moment?"

"Aye aye."

Ama had never had what one might call a tutor in the pugilistic arts. She was more of a self-taught expert, learning by trial and error and by being the biggest bully on her street. She had as much artistry to her attacks as a boar did, but both she and the boar could hit hard.

"Throw me a punch," she instructed, holding up her palms for targets. I gave her a couple, but they barely pushed back her elbows at all. "Come, you won't hurt me. Hit me."

"That's as good as I can do."

"Bullshit, hit me like you hate me."

She caught the next fist that I threw and shoved me back with as little effort as if I were a toddler throwing a tantrum. She frowned in thought and made me do it again.

"I see what's wrong," she said at last, raising her own fists. "Put your palms up."

I flinched backwards. "You're going to hit me?"

"Mouse..." she huffed. "Thicken your skin. Hands. Up."

I raised my palms up as targets, and Ama ducked down into a fighting stance. I could tell just by the way that she drew back her fist that it was going to hurt, and when she threw her whole shoulder forward and punched through my hand, it felt like a cannonball. I reeled, then spent what felt like several minutes pacing around and trying to shake out the painful, sizzling numbness that the strike left behind.

"There," Ama said, "Feel the difference?"

"Aye," I grumbled, although feeling and doing were different things.

Deciphering exactly how Ama did what she did was a painful, collaborative exercise, but we did begin to make progress. I learned how important it is to be grounded on my feet, when Ama unbalanced me and almost sent me flying off into the ocean. I learned that the legs are just as important as the arms when putting power behind a punch. She showed me the proper way to hold my fists, and to aim not just to touch against the target, but to punch through it to the back.

Ama thought more between days about how best to instruct me, and she came back to me with a new exercise to try every afternoon. The day after she taught me how to throw a good punch, she showed me tricks for how to move my feet efficiently—a little shuffle that could take me back and forth from my enemy. The next day, she commanded me to try to hit her. At first, I didn't put too much force into my attempt, because I didn't want to hurt her, but it quickly became apparent that I would be lucky if hitting her was ever going to be a real possibility. Ama was untouchable. She kept her left arm out in front of her, and whenever I tried to come in for an attack, she would push me back with a solid thrust of her palm, and keep up the distance.

"It's not fair," I complained. "Your arms are longer than mine."

That made Ama laugh. "They are not. Look. It's the difference between this,"—she first faced me straight-on and raised her arm so that her fingertips brushed my chin, "and this,"—she turned so that her shoulder came forward, and her hand reached all the way past my neck. "The difference of a shoulder-width can be the difference

81

between a hit and a miss. Turn so that one shoulder is out between you and your enemy. If someone is trying to cut you with a knife, you need to use your arm to protect the parts of you that can be seriously damaged. This,"—she tapped a white dagger scar on her forearm,"Is much better than this,"—she tapped a similar scar under her neck. "And if all your dancing around frustrates them and makes them throw their all into attacking, that's when you hit them with the big gut punch."

"So dancing around is good?" I asked, going over to my notebook to write it down. Whenever I did, Ama did her best governess impression, as she attempted to put her experiential wisdom into words (much to the enjoyment of those nearby who would sometimes stop and watch us fail to fight).

"It's surprise," she said. "That's how you defeat a superior opponent, a faster or a stronger opponent: through surprise. If you allow the fight to follow their plan, and you make a right and fair contest of it, then you will lose. The closer the fight goes to what they expect, to the way they're used to handling, the worse it is for you."

That was unfortunate for me, because my opponent-to-be was usually within spitting distance of these little training sessions, watching me out of the corner of his eye.

Jaks was unhappy with how things were progressing. When he had told me on the *Buenaventura* that he was going to beat a lesson into me, he had not envisioned a fight or a duel or anything of that nature. Now, after a few days of me training against Ama on the ship, what he'd intended to be a one-sided and private affair was becoming a public contest. Crewmates whispered all up and down the *Villainelle* about the upcoming fight, and even put bets on who they thought the victor would be. The news was spread in whispers to keep Toussaint,

Ama, and Socks from learning of it—any of whom might be tempted to step in and defend me—or Riley, who was a known blabbermouth.

It all made Jaks irate. "It's not going to be a fight," he kept saying.

In truth, Jaks was the kind of young man who took things too seriously, and had too inflated a sense of his own pride, which made him both very easy and very entertaining to provoke. The crew treated Jaks and myself as rivals because it made him bristle more than because they thought it was true. Yet, as the days went on, an aura of genuine excitement grew between us co-conspirators onboard the *Villainelle*, as we planned to make an event of it once we made landfall.

Zayne was the organizer of this occasion and the collector of bets. He knew of a drinking hole in Vera Cruz, off on a beach by the outskirts of the city, where, for just a few drops of silver in the barkeep's palm, we could stage a fight without drawing any unwanted attention from the Inquisition or the Acordada. Zayne also sometimes intruded upon my training sessions with Ama, to add a little bit of his own advice (as he was not exactly an unbloodied fighter himself).

"He's going to think low of you. You can use that," he said, glancing around to make sure that Jaks wasn't nearby. Ama was still there, so he didn't refer to Jaks by name, but only obliquely. "A man might see you and think he does not need to try. Might, if he were a prideful man, he might think it a matter of pride that he can't be too long, or use too much strength. He might fight hard from the start, spend all his strength running after you. Might tire out. Might, if he had a bit of anger in him, start making wide moves, and leave himself open. So...the run-away, the push back, and the surprise attack when the time is good."

"I've said all this already," Ama said grumpily. "If you're going to make yourself useful, come and put your hands up for new targets."

All of this dancing around reminded me of Toussaint when first we met, when Bad Weather ran up and down the railing in front of the storm, taunting the sea so that it would splash up against the side of the boat, just behind where he had been. Now I saw: he too had been battling against a stronger opponent. While I danced about out in front of Ama's reach or Zayne's, I imagined that I was like him, and tried to have fun with it. The fun helped.

We stopped by the Cayman Islands for supplies on our way to Vera Cruz. With an extra half-dozen Spanish mouths to feed, we'd eaten through most of our non-tack rations, and were now in dire need of more food. To pay for it, we planned on selling some of the more obviously valuable artifacts that we'd taken from the *Buenaventura*, but Ruiz the clerk begged us not to.

"Please, my superiors in Vera Cruz will pay you double. Triple!"

"I don't suppose you would be willing to sign a bill to that effect?" Socks asked wryly.

In the end, Toussaint and Socks went ashore with mostly Spanish coin, and only a couple of gold and silver Aztec relics; although those latter were brought along more to gauge their prices than to really be sold (and to drive up their value with Ruiz by panicking him, which it certainly did).

I took advantage of Toussaint's absence to take the curator aside. He was in a state of anxiety, but I had something to ask him.

"Signor Ruiz. I have been meaning to get your eyes on something," I said, and opened up my notebook. Inside was a facsimile that I had drawn, to the best of my recollection, of the mask that Toussaint had thrown into the sea.

I had tried to ask the first mate to share with me any more details about the mask, or about his history in general, and he had been so flighty as to immediately deflect and flee at the slightest mention of it. Even sideways comments set him on edge. They ruined his mood besides, so I had given up trying to pry it from him directly.

"Yes," Ruiz said, after taking the notebook and squinting at it up in front of his nose. "It is an image of one of the heathen gods."

"A god?" I asked. "What kind of god?"

"A common one," he said. "Often carved in their ruins."

"Do you know its name? Is it a big, important figure? What does it represent?"

"You should not give such care to this blasphemy," he warned me. "Even one such as yourself…" He looked at me with a kind of judgmental frown. "Should try not to fall further from grace."

I frowned right back at him. "Name," I commanded, and, when he still hesitated, I threatened, "Or do you want me to call over my friend, the big guy with all the piercings, and have him ask you?" and jerked my thumb in Zayne's direction.

"No, I do not," Ruiz said, and crossed himself. "It is Tlaloc. A false deity of rain and of harvest."

"Tlaloc," I repeated the name. "Tell me everything you know."

"I don't know anything," Ruiz said, affronted. "I walk in God's light; I do not look into dark corners. We took these idols from a heathen in Vera Cruz."

I asked, "Very well, who was the heathen?" For even if Ruiz knew nothing more about this mysterious figure, a heathen certainly should.

Ruiz seemed to be growing more uncomfortable with every question and kept looking like he might dart away if I let him. "The heathen…is called by some a sorcerer, an ungodly man. One to be avoided. It is my hope that he is already taken in and hanged."

"But what's his name?" I asked forcefully.

Ruiz grimaced, and reluctantly said, "Juliano Victoria. But I know nothing else but his name, and his reputation for dark things, I swear it, so take your blasphemies elsewhere."

I was both excited and nervous about bringing this news to Toussaint.

We took off from the Cayman port before the day was done and were soon back on the ocean. I found Toussaint on the aft deck. As much as he tended to be a smiling man, and a friendly man, he was also often quietly alone. He spent most evenings writing poetry on the back deck, looking out over the water. Because I liked to be with him, I sometimes intruded on his loneliness, but he didn't seem to mind. He always accepted and welcomed me with a smile.

I must admit that I was not a poet, nor an artist, but I spent these times with him attempting to develop both of these skills. In fact, some of the more poetical passages you've read in this book come straight from the journal that I worked on as I sat beside him, worrying about what I could say that he might find interesting.

This evening, I was drawing. Drawing him. I sat down in the crook where the side railing met the back and watched him, trying to figure out how to capture in a still image how his hair whipped about him in the wind. And when he caught me doing it, I blushed, and wouldn't let him look at it.

"Oh come now," Toussaint teased. "This is my face, is it not? Do you not think I have a right, as the plagiarized party, to see what it is that you have been making. A jester will mock to the king's face, you know."

"You are not a king and I am not a jester. I do not mock, I mark." My cheeks were hot, and my heart thump thumped in my chest.

"Alas, at least when my body is lost somewhere deep down in the sea, some memory will exist, even if it is only a mockery. Keep it safe for me."

I was surprised at his sudden sadness, and reached out to touch his arm. "Better to keep you safe for me."

"For you? Shall I be yours? You should know the devil owns my soul."

"I'll barter with him for it. I can find a prettier soul to offer."

"You think there is a prettier soul than mine?"

"Aye, and a humbler one. A less vexing one besides."

Toussaint laughed. "Well, it seems that my vexing tongue hasn't driven you away yet."

"Not at all," I said shyly. "But I should think that a less vexing soul would appeal more to Tlaloc."

At the mention of the god's name, Toussaint went as white as if I'd just revealed myself to be the devil himself. His lips went thin, eyes wide. Where a moment before he'd been lounging against the rail, leaning in towards me with curtained eyes and a playful smile, now he reared back with his legs bent as tight as springs.

"What was that you just said?" he asked me.

"I was talking to one of the passengers, from the *Buenaventura*," I stammered, anxious that I had been poking around behind his back. "I showed him this," I said meekly, and opened up my journal to where I had marked out the mask. Toussaint touched the paper with taut, disbelieving fingers.

"You...why?" he asked.

"He knew something. Tlaloc. The Aztec worshiped him, as a manifestation of rains—"

"I know, Mariah, I know what he is," he said with a tone of restrained anger. "And I know why he thinks he owns me."

"Then why will you never give me a straight answer?"

"It does not matter; there is nothing to be done. You cannot hit a god with a cannonball. I don't, Chéri, don't you know that I don't want you poking around in this?"

I crossed my arms at him, "Well I, for one, am not resigned to your death."

"So you hasten yours? Put your own self between mine and the sword? Merde." He sprung up to his feet.

"There might be something we could do," I told him. "You will never know if you continue to only run away."

"We? No, *I* will do something, you, I don't want you anywhere near—"

"You won't do anything," I cut in. "You think you're doomed."

"I *am* doomed. You do not need to be."

"Neither do you."

Toussaint faltered a step out of his rant. The part of him that didn't want to be doomed tripped over the rest of him, so that his eloquence failed him for once.

I stepped up to him, and said, in a pacifying tone, "There is a man in Vera Cruz named Juliano Victoria. He is the one who had collected all these artifacts..."

Toussaint, recovered from his trip, cut me off with a sharp gesture down towards the middle of the ship. "Do you see down there where the main mast meets the deck? How some of the boards there are as black and cracked as charcoal? We had to replace the last mast. Do you know why? It was hit by lightning. Lightning! With my...with Alice, up in the crow's nest." He shuddered, and pulled his cap down over his eyes, reliving some memory of that terrible night. "I couldn't...after that, I couldn't pretend that it was only a little bad luck. She was not the first one whose fate I have twisted with mine own, but I vowed that she would be the last, and I won't break that vow for you."

"That can't be your fault," I tried to say.

"How can you say that?" he asked. "You know it's real. All of it."

"Then it's Tlaloc's fault, not yours."

"Don't say his name!"

"If it truly is an old god, then there should be some way to appease it. A substitution, a quest, a ritual, I don't know. But I know that just running won't do anything."

Toussaint snapped at me. "If there is something to be done, then I will do it. If this Juliano knows something, I will find it out. I don't need you to be near it, to end up like that," and he pointed again at the blackened wood.

"I won't," I said. "I know that you think you're a better survivor than anyone else, and maybe you are, but I know how to run too. Don't you remember that we're the same? I can run just as you can, and I can vex too." Toussaint gave a snort of agreement to that. "Yes, exactly. I'm not to be underestimated either."

Toussaint was getting flustered, but his snort relieved his tension a bit, and he took a breath to restrain the rest of it. "Mariah, I know that you are a very tempting person to believe in, but the only way to know for sure if you will or if you won't die, is when you do. It is only a game of waiting. I will die. Someday soon, I will be caught, and I am sorry, but I won't help you follow me to my death."

With that, Toussaint departed for the main deck, back to levity and publicity, with his usual friendly smile forced onto his lips. Though it pained me to remain silent, I didn't bring up the issue to him again for the rest of our voyage.

When we came to Vera Cruz at last, the *Villainelle* was abuzz with excitement for our long-overdue respite at shore, but this excitement was tempered by wariness about our destination. Vera Cruz was the most important coastal Spanish city on the mainland. This was where the Spanish treasure fleet came to dock twice a year and gorge itself on as much gold and silver as it could carry with it back to the old world. The surrounding waters were among the best hunting grounds for pirates in the Caribbean, but the harbor itself was one of the best defended. The legendary fort of St. Jean D'Ulua—the fort that broke the fleet of Hawkins and Drake—menaced us from its bleak post in the middle of the bay, as a wide and gray compound of battlements and prisons. Their cannons pointed towards us, and we knew that if the inquisition decided to treat us as pirates and not saviors, then we would soon find ourselves rotting inside of one of those famous prisons.

We did not feel welcome, and we laid anchor with our masthead pointed back out to sea, ready to flee at the slightest provocation. Despite the letters that our Spanish tagalongs sent in to the port authority on our behalf, it took us far too long to secure a bill of harborage. Tensions were always high whenever an English ship came into a Spanish port, or vice versa, for while England was not currently at war with Spain, that was the exception far more than it was the rule, and sometimes an attack was the first word a colony received that the old powers were at war. Although we had come into port soon after sunrise, it was well into the late afternoon before we were given leave to come ashore.

We brought the *Villainelle* in to dock beside a ship three times its size and carrying ten times as many cannons. This neighbor ship was embossed with the name *La Sabueso*—'The Hound'—and it flew the flag of the Mexican Inquisition. Toussaint and Socks, along with our rescued Spanish Maroons, went down to the dock where they met with a retinue of inquisitors. I watched from the ship as Toussaint spoke to them. I could tell from his many animated gestures that he was nervous, and doing his best to spin a tale of heroism and rescue, rather than opportunism and extortion.

Whatever he said, it went well. Toussaint and Socks secured themselves an invitation to the inquisitor's estate for an impromptu banquet, and secured leave for the rest of us to spend the evening on shore. It was with great relief that we scurried ourselves away from the menacing eyes of the inquisitors and into the city. Ama and Riley kept watch on the boat, while everyone else—those of us who knew of the contest—went together as one raucous group to a place known as La Palapa.

La Palapa was unlike any bar that I had been to in English waters. The building had no real walls; only supporting pillars of wood that held up a roof of thatched palm leaves. La Palapa was set up by a beautiful beach with clean sand, well away from the bustle of the harbor. The bar was relatively empty when we came up in the late afternoon, but they were happy to have the business once Zayne showed the barkeep his silver. Soon, wine, rum, and beer were all flowing freely.

"Last chance to place your bets," Zayne said, touring around the open room as the sky grew orange. We would begin our contest when the sun set. Our crew was in good spirits now, and explained in Spanish to some of the local patrons at the bar how our "mad mouse" was going to serve the surly young Jaks a wallop. This was done with much laughter, and more wagers from both sides.

"It's not going to be a fight," Jaks said again, earning himself a mocking chorus from his crewmates, all repeating his best-known phrase.

I, meanwhile, with the day now upon me, was feeling less and less confident about myself. While Jaks wrapped his knuckles up in cloth, he stared across the way at me the whole time. People kept buying drinks for him (perhaps wanting to even out the fight by getting him drunk) but he barely touched them. I watched with a sinking feeling in my gut, ruminating on the worst that could happen.

Although I had been too wrapped up in my side of the argument at the time to show it, or even to process it, I had to admit that Toussaint's revelation about the girl in the crow's nest had shaken me. This god, spirit, demon or whatever it might be—Tlaloc—had the ability to call lightning down from the heavens, to smite someone who was only sitting in the wrong place at the wrong time, and here I was, willingly engaging in a fight with someone who wanted to kill me. I was more than tempting fate—I was provoking it! I started to feel less like a loss would mean bruises or broken bones, and more that it would mean my death.

Zayne came up to me bearing his own ball of bandages, which he began to wrap around my knuckles just as Jaks had done with his.

"You feeling good, Mouse?" he asked me quietly.

Jaks called at us, "She's not going to need those." Neither I nor Zayne responded, but another chorus of drunken derision for my surly opponent's bravado swallowed him up. Zayne kept wrapping my hands, unfazed.

I bent down towards him, so that only Zayne could hear me whisper, "If I wanted to call this off, what would that mean?"

Zayne faltered a bit, then resumed his wrapping.

"You are going to be good, Mouse. Just run around, then one big punch, yes? Don't let him in your head." He poked my forehead. "I've got money on you. You surprise him for me."

We went out to the beach behind the bar at sunset. The crew set out a circle of tall torches to mark out the arena for our battle, and lit them one by one as the sun sunk below the horizon. Jaks walked to the far end, where he started stretching out his muscular limbs, looking down his chin at me.

"I don't want to beat you down," Jaks said, cracking his knuckles and the bones in his neck. "But I will. If you only admit you were wrong, and apologize to me, then we can all go back inside, and nothing more needs to happen."

"Apologize for what?" I asked, clenching my hands at my sides. "You don't get to order me around. You're not better than me, even if you act like you are."

"I am better," he said flatly. "You, baby mouse, I've killed more men than you've kissed. I was born in hell, and I clawed my way out of it while you were sleeping soft in a feather bed at home." He shook his head out. "When I'm beating you down into the sand, I want you to think about how you brought this about. This isn't a game. None of this. This isn't make-believe playtime for little girls. If you don't take it serious, you die. I want you to think about that lesson, and be grateful when it's done."

The air was now purple and dark around us. The levity of the occasion dampened, as people around the ring caught on that Jaks hadn't been boasting for nothing, and he was fully prepared to crush me like a roach under his heel. The crowd quieted in anticipation. I shivered in the evening wind.

Zayne cleared his throat. "We begin on three. One. Two. Three."

It started too suddenly, and my muscles all seized up. As Jaks walked up to me, his gait was leisurely, as though I were a bundle of ropes that he had to come pick up and load onto the boat. His wide shoulders rolled as he walked, and his hands clenched and unclenched.

I jerked my fists up into a defensive stance and jumped my left foot in front of my right. The cloth wrappings bit into my palms, against my half-formed beginnings of callouses.

Jaks didn't bother to fight like Ama, feinting or pretending or guarding. He just came up to me and grabbed my arm. I saw the grab coming—he didn't hide it—but my arms froze in place, and I forgot to jump away backwards. He yanked me up, so that I balanced on my tiptoes in the sand, and drew back his fist.

"You're welcome," he said, and then he swung.

I raised a blocking arm by instinct, so that he smashed my arm into my face. The hit left me numb from elbow to fingertip. Jaks drew back his fist again.

As everything else fled from my mind, one of Ama's early lessons stuck hold. It was a lesson from before we even began fighting for what to do when a man comes at you alone in the dark—a weak spot to shoot for without mercy. Jaks was standing up straight, taking no defensive precautions. His knees were locked, his feet a shoulder-width apart. He was not ready for a counter-attack, so when I reared back with my knee and took my shot, it hit him straight and true.

The men in our audience all groaned, cringed, and laughed as Jaks dropped me and went down. I ran to the other side of the ring with my hands raised, ready for his next attack, but Jaks stayed on the ground writhing and cursing, oh, some very bad curses. Bad even for sailors.

"You ship-shape there, Jaks?" Zayne asked, and his voice held a mocking to it. "Stand up, kid, or she wins."

Jaks rose up on shaky legs.

"There you go," Zayne said.

"That was a dirty shot," Jaks spat.

I narrowed my eyes at him. "This isn't playtime for little girls," I mocked.

Jaks came charging at me with his shoulder forward and his fist raised for another very obvious attack. My body responded this time when I told it to duck, and he was not very light on his feet now, so

94

I danced around him and ran away. As he stagger-stepped after me, I could see him getting red in the face. I laughed at him, like Toussaint laughed at the storm.

"Come, come," I taunted. "Where's all that bluster from before? On no, you can't spout it anymore, is that it? I hit your nuts too hard, and now—whoop." I ducked and danced away as Jaks tried to grab at me again, giving him another laugh for good measure.

Between his big attacks, I gave Jaks a few exploratory jabs to the arms. I'm sure that they didn't hurt at all, but the mere fact that I could land a punch at all struck him with obvious surprise. He shook his head, and I jabbed at him again before he was done shaking it. I jabbed him twice more, with the same rhythm, getting him used to the weak left punch.

He went to trap my fifth punch with both hands, so that he could finally use his superior strength against me, but that's what I was waiting for. As he trapped my left, I gave him the strong right, straight through the little divot over his stomach, aiming to punch through his lungs and out the back. It hit right on target, and drove all the wind out of him at once.

Jaks wheezed, all breath gone, but he still had my left arm. With one hand on my wrist and the other on my shoulder, he swung my arm like a pickaxe into the sand, and the rest of my body followed. My face and shoulder smashed down into the ground, and grainy blood filled my mouth. If we were fighting on flagstones, the attack might have broken my neck.

Something snapped in me as I tasted my own blood and felt the nearness of my death. I plunged my free hand into the sand and flung it into Jaks' face. He cursed at me and closed his eyes, but wouldn't let my arm go. He smashed me into the sand again, and I heard something pop, and suddenly my arm wouldn't move at all. This smash was weaker than the first, however, as Jaks' breath had not come back to him, and he wobbled as if dizzy or drunk.

A heat flooded my senses. All that I remember thinking is that I wasn't going to let this prick kill me. I let out a primal war cry as I smashed my fist into his face, right under one of his closed eyes, and even with the bandages on my knuckles, the hardness of his cheekbones hurt my hand. His grip weakened, and I hit him again, and again, until he let me go. I scurried up to all fours, with one of the four dragging limply in the sand, and snarled, as Jaks kneeled over on hands and knees and struggled to get any air into his lungs. I pounced forward, reared back my leg, and smashed my boot as hard as I could into his belly.

Jaks fell to the side. He held up an arm weakly, like a shield, but I kicked him again, and this time after he fell over into the sand, he didn't move at all. I reared back to kick him a third time, but a set of arms wrapped around my torso from behind and lifted me up off the ground. I snarled and flailed on instinct.

"Woah woah woah," Zayne said, "That's enough there, Mouse, you got him, you win."

Stache, the ship sawbones, ran up and turned Jaks onto his back. He put his ear to the man's chest, then announced to the group, "He's out, but he'll live...with a hell of a headache."

"Thank god," Zayne exhaled. "Then it looks like we've got a Mad Mouse victory!"

My fever-rage faded as people cheered my victory. Zayne put me back down once I'd ceased struggling against him. I had sand scratches on my cheeks, and my head, neck, and shoulders hurt at every tiny movement. As Stache shoved my arm back into its socket, I yelled out, and afterwards gladly accepted liquor when it was offered to me.

My crewmates came up and bought me drinks all night long—drinks for Crazy Mouse, Mad Mouse, Wild Mouse. The more people said it, the more I liked the nickname. They bought for me even though I'd lost them money (most people who had bet on me only did so as a joke, and didn't put in more than a penny at most). I drank more than I'd ever had before, and I liked it more than usual, though I shoved most of the extra drinks off on Zayne. They called me Maddy too; I liked that one especially.

"I know one doesn't usually get to choose their nickname," I said to Zayne. "I didn't want to be a Mouse at all, but I'm happy enough...I can be okay with Mad Mouse. It makes Mouse better too, now that it's short for something."

"You are Mouse because this is the most I've ever heard you speak. Or squeak." Zayne laughed at his own joke.

"That's the beer," I said.

"Then drink more."

Zayne sat close with me for a long while, and even I, who had very little sense for such things, felt like he regarded me very positively indeed. He suggested that he could teach me a thing or two about wrestling some time, in private, and as I was blushing and stammering and trying to figure out how to refuse him kindly, Toussaint came into the palapa and made Zayne abruptly lean back and clear his throat.

Bad Weather hailed us cheerfully, although his presence here made my slowed wits spin in circles.

"What are you doing here?" I asked. I was in the habit of keeping this event a secret from him, and could not figure out whether or not that was still something that I should be doing.

"Why, my friend Zayne here, I hear has something for me."

"Aye," Zayne responded, and he passed Toussaint a big stack of silver coins. "The odds favored us."

I gasped at them. "You knew?"

Toussaint grinned. "It is a very small ship."

"But you didn't stop it."

"I did consider it," Toussaint said. "But in the end, I was too tempted to think that you would win, and I did not want to steal that victory from you."

I drunkenly fell into him with an embrace. "That means so much," I said into his chest. Zayne awkwardly backed away from us, but I didn't really take notice.

"Why so much?" Toussaint said lightly. "I'm a terrible gambler, you should know. But you're a good bet. And I should have learned by now not to underestimate you."

"That's true," I said, stabbing him in the chest with a finger, which he wrapped his hand around.

"I'm going to go to meet Juliano Victoria tomorrow," he said. "And I'd like you to come with me."

"Really?"

"Yes. I've been thinking very much about what you said to me, and it is true. I need to learn to run towards, not away, like you. I admire that about you, and I want to learn from you how to do it. So please do me the favor of coming with me."

I accepted tearfully, then took him to my bar of amassed beverages. I don't remember much of the evening after that; it all blurred into a celebratory haze. I know at some point that we must have borrowed a poncho, because Toussaint and I ended up laying out on one in the sandy beach together. He pointed to all the different constellations he knew and told me how we could find where we were on the ocean by looking at them. I mumbled to him some of the stories I knew about their mythical counterparts, and made up stories for those that I didn't know, so that we both laughed at the foolishness my inebriated mind came up with.

He mentioned that he had something important that he had been meaning to tell me, but by then I was already most of the way asleep.

Six for Deceit

I was basting in love, with my head on his shoulder, when the sun rose in the morning. This love was a warmth that had its home in my chest, but which stretched out to the tip of every extremity and radiated buzzing happiness from each drop of blood in my veins. Love was the warm bath that I simmered in, and it smoothed out the other sensations of the world so that the sand was soft and the breeze gentle. I had never before since the day I was born felt that level of safety and comfort, and I was no more prepared for the precipitous fall from joy to sorrow that was coming for me than I had been as a babe, when forced from the safe darkness of the womb to taste cruel reality for the first time.

Toussaint had draped his coats overtop us as blankets, so that we might have some protection from the elements through the autumn night. He always wore many stylish layers at a time, and this was the first that I'd glimpsed even a window of his chest, in the v of his silk shirt. My hand was already curled atop his sternum when I awoke, and I pet the skin there with trepidatious curiosity. It was as smooth and soft and hairless as his cheeks, which were bare as always of even the shadow of a beard.

My hand brushed up against a bandage which was wrapped tightly around his chest. I followed its edge under his shirt to where it passed under his arms, and everywhere that it pressed in, the skin curled around it with old, yellow bruises. A fear wriggled itself into my cozy love cocoon and made my breath tighten. I traced the seam between chest and bandage back to its center, where the strap made a shallow bridge between two mounds of constrained breast tissue.

I sat up suddenly, and the movement made him stir. He stretched out luxuriously, smiling, before he opened his eyes and saw the look on my face. He followed my gaze, which was affixed on his chest, and suddenly realized what it was that I was looking at.

His happiness curdled to horror in a moment, and he cursed and fumbled to pull the coats back over his shoulders. He curled over and shrunk himself into a ball, as if to hide what I had already seen. He looked at me in dismay, and although I waited for him to explain, his mouth opened and closed without finding the words.

Confused, and too dizzy to decide yet on another emotion, I asked him, "Were you ever going to tell me?"

"I don't...like...to talk...about it." he spoke in gasping breaths, as though frozen.

"I thought you were an honest man? Evidently, you're neither of those things."

He gasped at me like he was the one betrayed. "I..." he stammered, "can we...just...shit." He looked like I'd shot him through the chest. I had never seen him so small and pained; he looked so unlike who he was supposed to be.

My freefalling heart hit the floor. That heart had spent the last few hours climbing up, up, up the mountain of hope, thinking, yes, maybe I am going to be good enough for him after all, and then, in a moment, it turned around, convinced that not only was that not going to happen, it was never even a possibility. I feared in that moment of anxious panic that it had been a foolish endeavor from the beginning. It had been pointless, stupid, fruitless, vain...

"Explain," I demanded of him.

"I'm not...it's..." he failed to speak, and I lost my patience.

"Why," I asked tearfully. "Why, why, on earth, why have you been pretending all this time?"

"Why is it that you are the upset one?" He asked me. "I'm sorry, I...You went poking around! I wanted to tell you on my own time, at my own pace, and I wasn't yet ready..."

"When were you going to be ready? You and I have been alone together perhaps a dozen times now, and never once did I think...never did you say, hello, bonjour, thought you might want to know, just a small note: I've got teats."

That was a spiteful thing to say. I regretted it immediately, when I saw how it shot him through again with pain. I didn't understand, and confusion bred anger.

"You..." he gasped, pained. "How can you say that? I am not doing this to hurt you."

"How am I supposed to react?" I snapped. "You lied to me. You let me...fucking...fall for you." There. I said it. I slapped him with it. "Was it some cruel joke...all of it?"

"I told you it was a bad idea," he said with a wince. "It hurts people to be around me."

"Well thank you so much for keeping that promise." I spat. "I would never have...what would I have done? Nothing needed to be done if I knew of it. I'd simply know not to...I would have known how

I was supposed to think of you. Why did you need you disguise it from me? Why make a game of it with me?"

"It is not a disguise, it is not a game, this is what I am saying," he said. "It is only who I am. I am Toussaint."

"Oh god," I despaired. "That's not even your real name."

"It is!" His expression contorted into anger. "I am him. This is who I am. I have chosen it. I have lived with it. I..." He clapped a hand over his face and took a steadying breath. "I am sorry. Really, this is not how I planned for this to go." He took up his cap from the gray sand of our dawn-lit beach and wrung its brim in his hands, not looking at me. "I wanted to explain to you...you know...your queen...Elizabeth...of England. She once said that although she had the weak and the feeble body of a woman, she had the heart and stomach of a king. That is me." He hit himself in the chest emphatically. "I have the heart of a king, and the stomach as well. I have always had a king's heart; it was just put in the wrong chest."

I didn't understand. I sputtered disbelieving sounds into the air, and he stood up. He came at me with passion behind his words, trying every way he could to convince me he spoke the truth.

"Look," he said, "when I was a child, I had dreams of going into the forest and finding a fairy who could turn my body into a man's, and it was beautiful. I just thought of it as a fantasy, but the thing about fantasy is that the more that you hold it in your heart, the more it becomes real. I snuck out in the clothes of a man, and the strangers of the quay treated me as a man, and I learned their trades like a man, and I did good manly work under a new name and felt proud about that life in a way that I never had living as a woman. It felt like that was the truth, and the lie was the life that I came back to at night, putting on skirts for my father. That wasn't me. It never had been. My true self is a man: Toussaint."

I stared at him, trying to grasp at what he said, but my head was saturated with thoughts already, and all of it was too much to hold. It was all too much, and it was all at once. None of it changed, to me, what I saw as the fundamental issue: that he had let me fall in love with him, even though he was a woman.

"But why now?" I asked, my voice straining with that pain. "Why still? I do man's work; I wear man's clothes. So does Ama. I don't tell people I'm a man."

"But I am a man, you understand? I can't explain the way it feels to someone who doesn't feel it."

"But why?"

"Why not?" he asked, growing more upset the more that he failed to make me understand. "Why not feed my king's stomach? Why force it down a way it doesn't want to go? I am a free man."

"But..."

"But what, Mariah?" He snapped. "I told you: this is what I am. I will not change, not for you, not for anyone. I told you it hurts to be near me, and if you can't, then you are free to leave."

"Fine," I huffed, rising in response to his anger. "Then I will." And I made to stomp off in a huff.

"Mariah!" he grabbed my wrist before I could go. "I'm sorry. Don't hate me for this. Do you hate me for it?"

"Toussaint..." I shuddered as I thought again how I didn't know his name. I yanked my arm away. "I can't hate you. I don't know you."

I looked and walked away. I was cruel. I denied him like Peter and left him alone in his despair. I glanced back before I left the beach completely. He was on his knees, with his hands dug into the sand, shoulders shaking. I hardened my pity with rage and turned towards the dockyard.

I was hurt (though not so hurt as Toussaint), and confused, and drenched in the sour aftereffects of alcohol. I didn't understand how to fit his secret with the world that I thought I knew, and, at its base, there was nothing that he could say that would make me not feel like a fool. If my life was a play, and someone was watching it unfold, I imagined how they must have laughed at me. I thought of the irony with which the audience must have mocked my swooning, and my pathetic mistaking of friendship for romance. I was like the peasant woman from As You Like It, who had been chasing after Ganymede while everyone in the audience knew, obviously, that Ganymede was only Rosalind in a beard, and she had been trying to shake me off this entire time. They would be laughing at me for my childishness, and, at the end of the play, the worst bit is, I was going to be left to marry the shepherd because that's how all these stories end, in marriage or death, and a comedy is still a tragedy to the one at the butt of the joke.

By the time that I returned to the Villainelle, I was far down my well-trod road of melancholy. The ship was preparing, in the chilly and hazy morning, to load itself up with supplies. My crewmates grumbled in various levels of bottle-ache, and the work was slow-going. Ama, who was sober and well-rested, made it clear that she expected the same level of work from these sodden trolls of the morning as she did from her usual crew.

"That's not your bed, Gopher," she shouted out to the young man draped over a barrel, whose seaweed-oily hair hid a green face. "And if you're going to spew your gut again, do it into the water."

I joined the others, hoping that physical exertion might help take the drain off of my mood, but it did not. John and Zayne offered me their friendly congratulations again, but I was too haunted to accept them. I remembered how they had put me up against Jaks with jokes, and wondered if there was a similar betting pool going on somewhere about Toussaint, and how long it would take me to discover that he was never, ever going to love me the way that I loved him. These poisonous thoughts and others kept me on the verge of tears as I silently carried small boxes back and forth from the dock.

Our work was hindered at every turn by the inquisition, who pried open the crates for inspection aboard our ship, and then a second time once we had deposited them onto the dock, as if we could have snuck in contraband in the couple dozen steps from one place to the next. The inquisitors were not welcome on our ship, but they made themselves welcome. No door was closed to the inquisition in their own country, so they pushed their way into our hold and took every good of questionable moral standard which we had not quite managed to sequester before they arrived: alcohol, playing cards (sometimes marked with erotic images), and books. They took every book—sea-stained as they might be—which was of French or English origin, suspecting them of bringing seditionary philosophies into the colony.

"This is robbery," Socks exclaimed to them, red faced, as they took his stack of soggy books away down the gangplank.

"Your soul shall thank us," said the inquisitor Samuel, who carried the books with his nose wrinkled back against imagined baleful fumes which may have come off of them. "These texts are ungodly things. Take care not to join them on the pyre."

Socks huffed at their back, but even as upset as he was, he knew better than to challenge the inquisition in their own city. "I hope they choke on the smoke," he growled, and spread the word to speed up our repairs so that we might leave port as soon as possible.

When Ama was in her at-work state of mind, she never gave much attention to the well-being of those under her management (at least, not as much as she arguably should). The work was always so large in front of her eyes so as to crowd out anything else, so no matter how much I might have thought that I was being obvious, or even excessive, with my displays of unhappiness, it wasn't until the work reached a lull, and every box was set away, that Ama noticed me as my sad puddle-self on the back of the boat, dripping melancholy into the bay.

"Is something the matter back here?" she asked me.

"I'm fine."

"Very well," she said, and walked away. A little while later, she came back and sat on a crate across from me. Businesslike, and ready to tackle the issue head on, she asked again, "What's the matter?"

Her disposition tarred up my teeth. "Never mind it."

"Is it Jaks?" she asked me, folding up her arms. "Don't fret about the lad. He needed a humbling."

I balked. "What? How did you know about it too?" The events of the previous day felt far away, but even still...

"You're not half as subtle as you think, Miss Mad Mouse," Ama said with a smirk. "I have to admit, you did better than expected. I'm proud of you."

"Thank you," I said with a confused bit of pleasure, though I was far away from smiling.

"God bless," Ama said, "But if that's not it... Toussaint?"

My stomach did a tumble at his name, and I hid my face in my arm.

"Come now, Mouse," Ama said. "He's a vexing fellow, yeah?"

I snorted.

Ama wasn't very good at what she was trying to do. There is plenty that she could have said to right my perspective. She could have told me then about her own struggles with similar issues, and particularly her shared history with Toussaint, when they were both younger and figuring out their hearts and stomachs. She could have told me about her lover back in Tortuga, and her journey to accepting the part of herself that loved to wrap her arms around another woman's waist. But Ama was not that gentle, nor that patient.

"I take it he told you his big secret?" she asked me. I sullenly kept my mouth closed. "Well, it's natural to be disappointed."

"I'm not disappointed," I said bitterly, even though that was part of what I was feeling.

"Yeah? You seem upset."

"I'm not." Though I was that too.

"Well, guess I'm wrong. Look who's all fine." She clapped her hands on her thighs and got up, reaching the end of her patience already. "Go take a lie down, Mouse. You'll feel better after."

"You could have warned me," I bit at her.

"First, I did warn you," she bit back. "Second, I'm not your damn mother here to tell you who to fuck. You're a grown woman, for Christ's sake, and that means you get to fall in love with the wrong man. It's how it goes."

"I'm not in love with her," I said bitterly.

"Woah," Ama reared, and stomped down next to me. "Look at me," she commanded, "I'm going to let that one go, because you're new to this, but don't you damn forget to call him 'him' or you're going to find yourself off the ship, understand me? People choose this life, dangerous as it is, to get away from shits trying to tell them what they're allowed to be. When you risk your life for your livelihood, you get to be who you want to be, and fuck who you want to fuck, and I'll fuck up anyone who says different, even if it's you, Mouse. That's why I'm here. And Toussaint as well. Got it?"

"Yes maam," I said, deflating, and feeling ashamed at having made her talk so severely to me.

"Good," Ama said. "Before today, you were blind with love for the fool. What kind of puddle-shallow love was that if you treat him like this now?" She shook her head in disgust and left my sad corner of the deck behind.

My shame worsened in the wake of Ama's lecture. I spent the rest of the afternoon tumbling thoughts around inside my head, each chasing the last from it for fear of its implications. I didn't want to think about how I had really never loved another man in my life the way that I loved him. I didn't want to think about what made him different from the suitors who had come up to me in my youth. I didn't want to think about any of it.

I earned myself an aching head and little else from the exercise, which grew worse as my attitude began to migrate from one of disbelief to one of belief. I knew Ama to be a blunt and honest woman; she didn't have the same habit of charm as Toussaint did, and I trusted her word more than his. She acted like Toussaint meant everything that he said, and that meant that he hadn't lied to me at all, which made me the rotten one. He was a man, for himself, and that was all. It was hard for him to tell me, but he'd meant to, and I'd discovered it too soon and made it all go terribly. My new shame wasn't at being the fool, but at being the villain, which was worse.

By the time dinner came around, I only knew that I needed to speak with him again, without falling victim to my own disbelief. I didn't know what I was going to say, other than that I needed to apologize to him. I figured that I would know in the moment what needed to be said. I watched the dock vigilantly for him all through the day, but he never returned.

El Sabueso, the inquisition ship with which we had shared a dock, took themselves to the other side of the bay, to the famous fort of D'Ulua, and there they loaded themselves up with cannon-shot and prisoners from within the fort. Socks told Riley—our most eagle-eyed sailor—to keep a lookout, and to report at the first sign of those cannons being loaded, or at all positioned to levy fire upon us.

"Nonsense to fire at us now, isn't it?" Riley asked. "They just paid us, didn't they?"

"They have no sense," Socks growled. "Sense is their enemy." The captain, who was usually slow to anger, seemed to be just as slow to come back down from it. He was nearly as red-faced as when the inquisitors had bullied their way into his hold. "The inquisition is a corrupt and evil organization, and I will yell so to the sea once we are back safely upon it."

I skipped dinner in order to maintain my vigil, so Ama brought me up a bowl from below. "You need to eat," she said, as she had many times before.

"I'm not hungry," I muttered, but it touched me that, even though she was upset with me, she still wanted to make sure that I wouldn't neglect myself, so, after a stubborn moment, I added a, "Thank you," and took the bowl. It was well-stocked with roasted chicken, fresh tomatoes, and onions—all the victual comforts of a civilized harbor.

"We're leaving in the morning," she said to me gruffly.

"Has Toussaint come back yet?" I asked.

She frowned at me. "I don't think he is coming back."

I froze, with food pouched in my cheek. "Because of me?"

Ama leaned back against the aft mast, folding her arms, and said, "It's what he does."

"But we can't leave without him, right?"

"It's his habit. Gets in his head when things go wrong, about how he's going to wreck us with his bad luck, so he has to go spend it all somewhere else. Nonsense, if you ask me. He's just unhappy." She spoke not towards me, but off the side of the boat, as if looking out for Toussaint to come and prove her wrong. "He'll eventually find his way back to us. Might be weeks or months before we run into him on Tortuga, but he always makes it back."

"I'm sorry," I said, guilt-laden. "Maybe I could talk to him?"

She shook her head. "There's nothing you can say. He's stubborn, and won't listen to reason."

"I can't just...I need to apologize to him at least," I said. "Do you know where he is?"

I did not expect Ama to point me toward the biggest church in Vera Cruz, but that's where she said he would be. The basilica was large and immaculately white, with one big tower in the corner of a large compound. It looked very new, as it had been rebuilt less than a decade ago, after the last one had burned in a fire.

I found Toussaint inside the chapel of our lady of absolution. He was sitting on the low stone stair beside the altar, with his head bent down, and his hair hung down over his face like a mop. He slouched with all of his limbs hanging weakly at the joints, all fallen together like bones stuffed into a sack.

My footsteps echoed on the stone tiles, making Toussaint look up at the sound. His mouth twitched weakly as he said, "Bonjour."

I flinched back into the doorway, with my fingers curling against the doorjamb. Words failed me at first, even a greeting.

"I never took you for a godly man," I said at last. My mouth was dry.

"Indeed?" Toussaint asked, with short laugh at himself. "I do admit, this was my first penance in a long while. Believe it or not, I was a very good Christian once upon a time. Although I suppose, according to you, I wasn't a godly man then either."

"I'm sorry," I said to get it out. I edged out from behind the doorway, with my hands stumbling over each other, like my words, in meaningless gestures. "I shouldn't have...I was only trying to hurt you with what I said, and I shouldn't have. I was just...no, I shouldn't make excuses. I'm sorry." My hands fell as I dropped my apology, feeling even as I said it that it was insufficient.

"Thank you," he said softly, sounding wrung out. "I do not blame you for misunderstanding. We are only human; it is in our nature to hurt one another. I am sorry as well, for my fear and my anger, which made things all the worse. We cannot see each other soul to soul. We only have human action and human word with which to share ourselves, and these things are sometimes sharp. I should have known better by now what to expect."

I felt like my apology had not been received with the gravity with which I had meant it. "Do you hate me for what I said?" I asked. "You should. It was...I am sorry. I didn't know what to believe."

Toussaint sighed, but seemed a little happier at the second apology. "Thank you for saying that, but I know, really, it was bad luck that made us hurt each other. It made the truth come out in a way that hurt you, and then you hurt me, and I hurt you. Let's stop that cycle, yes? Let's start over."

"Yes," I said, amazed at his open heart. I shuffled my feet and said, "The ship is leaving in the morning. Are you going to come back?"

"I do not know," Toussaint said. He looked up, far away, over the head of the Virgin Mary. "I feel as though a run of bad luck is coming on, and I do not like to catch up the ship in it."

"I don't want to leave you behind."

"It is not so big a thing." Toussaint waved a dismissive hand. "I will be back, so long as death does not find me first."

"But what of Victoria?" I objected. "You told me that I could come with you to find a solution to all of this. Or has that changed now?"

"Still you want to?"

"Of course I do!"

He gave me a strange look. "You are always coming towards me, even as I try my hardest to stay away. You find me in my solitude and you bring me company."

"I'm sorry if that isn't what you want."

"No, I am grateful for it. My exile is self-imposed. I choose it not because I like it, but because I fear the suffering that I will bring to those I care about. That you know that and still choose to be near me...I am grateful for it, even though it shames me to make you welcome. You are kind, and generous, and brave. I am...very glad that you have not abandoned me after all."

My heart twinged in a familiar way, and I scrambled to bury my love as it rose up again. I felt like none of those things he called me—I felt like a villain and a monster and a fool all at once—and it was absolutely incredible to me that he could forgive so easily and still see something beautiful in me when I saw nothing of the sort.

"No, you, you are too good." I came and sat on the stair next to him. I grabbed his arm, and said, again, "I'm sorry. I've been...I know myself to be...distracted by the way that I fear things to be. I feared how much I may have dreamt you, and how much was real. I was wrong and cruel and you shouldn't forgive me."

Toussaint put his hand atop of mine, and didn't say anything else for a while. We sat together in silence, until at last he spoke:

"My father was a godly man. Everyone said that he was a saint. There was a story, you see, from when I was only a baby, that he'd spent every day and night in a chapel just like this one, praying for something to save our settlement. Then, one night, in the midst of a storm that threatened to ruin us for the final time, he ran alone out of the chapel and into the fields. They say that he met with God there, and pled with him, and once the next morning came, lo and behold, our harvest was spared. The rains were life-giving; the winds were kind. God heard his devotion and transformed the craggiest rock in the Caribbean into one of its richest plantations, almost overnight. I loved and admired him very much for that story, when I was younger, before I learned the truth.

"It wasn't God who did it. My father was fed up, you see, with going to the chapel every night and getting nothing back. He was a desperate man, and willing to deal with whatever put itself before him. So instead of with God, he dealt with the demon that he found in the storm: this Tlaloc, or Chaac. Demon or spirit or god, it offered him a covenant. It promised to bless our island with the one good rain, not the four bad ones, in exchange for the sacrifice of his oldest son.

"You must imagine, my father thought he'd stumbled into some good luck. Because he didn't have a son; he had a daughter. Or so he thought. Fate is a funny thing."

Toussaint took a deep, steadying breath, and hid his face in his hand as he continued.

"This, you see, this is why it is my fault. I know the solution to my curse. There is something I could do to end it. I would only need to recant my name, trade son back for daughter, and the god would have no claim on me. But I can't do it." He grabbed himself by the chest with a claw so tight it could tear into his skin. "This is who I am, and I won't sacrifice it for a god nor for my father neither. I would rather fight to my dying breath than relinquish myself to that false life. This is the depth of my shame. My selfishness. I choose the fight; I choose violence; it is on my head, don't you see? Everything—every pointless injury and death—it is all my fault. I am the one who should not be forgiven."

I was amazed, when I looked at him, that I could ever have thought this man didn't mean what he said to me. He spoke with his pain written on his face, frank and honest, which turned the veins in his temples blue and drew tears from his eyes.

"It's not your fault," I said. "How could you think the guilt lies with you? It lies on your father's shoulders, or on the demon's, never yours."

Toussaint laughed to himself. "This is not what the priest of this church said. I told him my story in confession, and he told me to seek forgiveness for my blasphemy and my sodomy, like those are the things I'm sorry for." He hung his head in his hand. "Made me feel like I should be giving up and dying already."

I took him by the hand, so that he couldn't use it to hide anymore, and pulled it into my lap. "As quick as you are to forgive me, you're too slow to forgive yourself. I am sorry, again, that I didn't understand before, but I do now. I believe you. I see you, soul to soul, and I know: you couldn't have done elsewise. Do you really think Bad Weather is such an easy name to recant? Not the Bad Weather I know. Not the Toussaint I know neither."

Toussaint wiped a tear off onto his unrestrained forearm. "Do you really think that I should not change? You called it a disguise. You said you didn't know me."

"And I was wrong. I know you. You are Toussaint Dupuis. You are the man who fights a god, and laughs as he's doing it. And I want to fight him with you."

Our words faltered then. So did my worries. We only sat together for a time. While I held him, I returned to a warmth that was both like and unlike that of the early morning. It was the warmth of two people huddling together in a ramshackle shelter while a storm rages outside: the strange phenomenon whereby two individuals, who are each themselves cold, can nevertheless make the other warm just by curling up against them. I felt warm. It was a warmth that had its home in our hearts, but which spread out to every extremity. It was a warmth we shared between us. Soul to soul.

Seven for Victory

E vening folded well into night by the time Toussaint and I left the discomfort of the church floor for the shadowed streets of Vera Cruz. The city decreed that its residents must maintain light in their windows throughout the night every night—by candle or lantern—to brighten the streets. Our path was half-lit, and somewhat spooky, but with enough to see our feet by as we slipped down the dark boulevard towards the home of the sorcerer Juliano Victoria.

"It is not good manners," Toussaint grumbled, "To stop by, un-expected, at night, without even a bottle of brandy to make your company more pleasant."

"It's too late to buy brandy; our company will have to be enough."

"Back on the ship..." he stopped at the look I gave him. "Never mind."

If we were to go back to the *Villainelle* to pick up a bottle of brandy, then we would find another excuse, and another thing in the way, until we would put it off forever. With our departure on the horizon, this was the last opportunity to make the mystic man's acquaintance, and learn if he knew of any means by which one could combat the face that had frightened Toussaint so badly.

"Bad manners, Bad Weather, he'll have to forgive them," I said, and dragged Toussaint along.

The Victoria estate did not look like the kind of place that would belong to an iconoclast. I might have expected a rundown hermit hut on the edge of town, smelling of sulfur, but instead, what I found was just one of many white houses on a row: big, blocky, and sagging down in one corner. A lantern hung up in its top window, and although the downstairs curtains were drawn shut, light seeped out from the cracks between fabric and stone. Someone was home.

When I knocked on the door, the whispered conversation on the other side stopped abruptly; it was only by its sudden silence that I became aware that it had ever existed. I knocked again, and the silence gave way to the muffled sound of shifting fabric.

"Hello?" I asked the door as I knocked again. "Signor Victoria?"

When the door opened up a crack at last, a quarter of an unshaven face appeared before us in the slot between door and jamb. The face had a blocky chin with a patchy week's growth of beard and a surly expression.

"[Who are you?]" the man asked in a coarse Spanish dialect. I was taken aback, and Toussaint slipped in between us.

"[Apologies for the late hour,]" Toussaint said quickly, in much better Spanish than mine. "[We are foreigners, here to speak with a Signor Juliano Victoria. Are you he?]"

He glared at Toussaint and said, "No."

"[Is this his home?]" I asked, also in spanish.

He answered with a bit of Spanish that I didn't fully understand, but which gave the gist of a complicated affirmation. This was the right place.

"[Is he here?]" I asked.

"[No, he is not.]"

"[Ah, that's our bad luck]," Toussaint said jovially, and he made to leave, but I wouldn't move no matter how he tugged against the back of my coat.

"[Do you know where he is?]" I pressed on.

The man's expression hardened, and the bristles around his lips squirmed unhappily. "[What do you want from him?]"

"[It is nothing that cannot wait...]" Toussaint started.

"[He knows about old gods, yes?]" I pushed. "[We need his help.]"

The man behind the door ground his jaw, and said, "[No, thank you, we don't know anything about that.]"

He started to close the door on me, but I stuck my foot in the way to stop it.

Toussaint hissed at me in English, "Mariah, you cannot speak of such things in the street in New Spain," but I was not afraid.

"[We know that he is a sorcerer,]" I pushed on. "[We know that he brought Aztec artifacts into the city.]" The man's expression darkened further, and Toussaint tugged on my arm. "[Where did he get them? Who does he know? I need to speak with him, and I'm not leaving until I do.]"

The doorman grimaced, and looked back over his shoulder.

A second voice called out from within the house, with a command: "[Zaragoza, open the door.]"

The surly Zaragoza did as he was told. Inside, a second man, whose sallow cheeks were sparsely speckled with blonde bristles, sat on a stool and pointed an old, brass-cast musket at us.

"Come in," he said, flatly, in English.

Inside looked like the aftermath of a particularly violent robbery. Splintered chunks of wood were strewn all across the floor, along with wide spatters of spilt ink and stuffing from every seat-slitted cushion. A third man sat in one of the eviscerated chairs with his fingers steepled together, glaring at us in thought.

"Weapons on the table," commanded the blonde man with the musket. "Slowly."

The table that he gestured to was low-lying, and ink-stained. It appeared to be set for a friendly gathering, with three half-empty tumblers of liquor and a dish full of olive pits. Toussaint withdrew his two pistols from his bandolier, as well as his cutlass, and laid them down by the olive plate. I followed suit with my cutlass, and once we were done, the gunman commanded us to back ourselves up to the wall.

"Who are you?" he demanded. "Names, sir."

"Toussaint Dupuis is my name," Toussaint said, calm and affable, with his open palms held up in the air. "You may have heard of me by the name Bad Weather? No? My companion here is Mariah, and we both together sail upon the *Villainelle*."

"What brings your ship to Vera Cruz, sir?"

Toussaint smiled, nervously. "Ah, that appears to be a matter of ill fortune. A ship from your harbor, bound for Spain, ran aground near Bermuda in a storm. We happened to stumble across the wreckage, save some maroons, and take some of their stranger and more valuable cargo back here to Vera Cruz, for what we were assured would be a large reward. We only arrived here yesterday, and we are leaving tomorrow."

"So what does that make you?" Asked Zaragoza, who came around to poke curiously at our weapons. "Scavengers?"

"On occasion," said Toussaint. "Also smugglers."

"Mercenaries?"

"You could say so."

As Toussaint took charge of the conversation, I darted my eyes around the room, trying to gather more information about who these people were. None of them looked like a sorcerer, and neither did the home looked like it belonged to one. I saw a great deal of paper debris, in shreds and trampled under black footprints. I followed the trails of smeared black ink to a bulky piece of furniture in the back corner, shrouded over by a hastily-thrown white sheet, but not so well as to hide it completely. Having lived above a bookbinder's shop for most of my life, I recognized, even from the one small corner that stuck out, the hidden printing press.

A broken printer, and evidence of an invasion. What did it mean?

"So why are you here?" asked the third man, who looked the most haunted of the lot. He had darker skin than the other two, and thin black hair in what was once a tight style, but had not been properly attended to in some time. His eyes were heavily lidded; his clothes, disheveled. "This house. How did you hear of it?"

"And keep it brief," added Zaragoza, taking up one of Toussaint's pistols and pointing it towards its owner.

Toussaint shrugged, like he had been asked an embarrassing question at a dinner party. "Why, the ship we found, it just so happened to be carrying these artifacts, which we had some questions about, some interest in, for our own purposes, and when we asked the port authority from whence they came, they pointed us in this direction." He glanced around nervously, and towards the door. "We did not know that we were interrupting an event, and I do apologize for that."

"You've caught us at a troubled time," said the haunted-looking man.

The gunman narrowed his eyes. Looking like he might pull the trigger, just to be careful.

"We only come by stumbling," Toussaint told him. "I must say, if there is something that you think we ought to know, I assure you that we know nothing, and would be more than happy to simply turn around and forget that we were ever here."

I slid my gaze across the tilted bookshelves, which were largely empty, save for a bible and a couple of Spanish religious texts, as well as a shrine to some Catholic saint whom I did not recognize. It was a suspiciously shallow collection for a home with a printing press of its own; what happened to the rest of it? Who goes into a home in the middle of Vera Cruz, destroys a secret printing press, searches voraciously, and takes books of all things?

One clear answer came to mind.

"We aren't with the inquisition," I ventured. "Look." I held out in front of me the rough-cut jade medallion which I had taken from the *Buenaventura*. The medallion's look was that of a peaceful woman's face, with slitted eyes and a soft kind of smile. It made me feel at ease. "I pulled this from the wreckage myself. It's one of his. I came with the intention of returning it, in exchange for his help."

The gunman removed his hand from the trigger. "Give it here." He took the medallion roughly, frowning, then tossed it to the haunted third man on the chair. In Spanish, he asked, "[Is it his?]"

The sitting man dangled the jade by its cord up in front of his eyes. He squinted at it, like one does when a memory lingers at the tip of their recollection.

"[It could be,]" he said as if to himself.

"[It doesn't matter,]" Zaragoza said roughly, speaking so rapidly that I could hardly follow what he was saying. He spoke to his friends as if we weren't there. "[She could have gotten it straight from their office.]"

"[But why wouldn't they send it to Spain with the rest of it?]" asked the gunman.

"[For this, to trick us,]" said Zaragoza.

"[They don't need to trick us,]" said the haunted man, still looking at the dangling medallion. "[They took everything—broke everything—already.]" He caught the medallion in his fist, and clenched it there. "[No, I think they are who they claim to be.]"

The gunman lowered his musket, but Zaragoza was slower to back down.

"[This does not mean that we should listen to them,]" he said. "[They are mercenary. They could be bought off. Your father didn't say a word, the whole month he rotted in D'Ulua; they're desperate to find something to bring down on you...]"

Toussaint said, "Sirs, we do not need anything from you, we have not seen anything, we only need to leave with the apology of a lifetime."

"No," Zaragoza said. "First, explain your business to me. Why do you need to speak to old Victoria?" Toussaint made to answer in his long way, but Zaragoza jabbed at his chest with the pistol to keep him quiet. "No. I want to hear it from the girl."

I smiled, for no good reason, and said, "It is a matter of a curse that needs breaking. There are a lot of good reasons to seek a sorcerer."

The haunted man laughed at that: a dark chuckle with more pain than mirth.

"[Of course]," he said. "[You wouldn't leave my home alone when he was here, why would you cease now?]" He glared at us, and said in English both slow and deliberate, "My father is gone. Gone for good. The inquisition snapped him up."

"The sorcerer is your father?" I asked.

"He's not a damn sorcerer," said the younger Victoria, hitting the table so that our guns rattled.

"He has a reputation..." I started.

"He's a fool, that's what he is," Zaragoza interrupted. "A fool who doesn't know when to keep quiet. They're going to burn him for a sorcerer, but that doesn't make it true."

"[It didn't matter what he was,]" muttered the gunman. "[It was only an excuse to come at us: reasonable men.]" And he glanced guiltily towards the dented printing press under its shroud.

"[They wouldn't have that excuse if it weren't for these idiots who keep calling what he does magic,]" Zaragoza said, waving his weapon towards Toussaint and me again.

"How do you know he's not magic?" I asked.

Victoria looked sour. "Bah. He's a head-cracked mystic. He's made claims to shamanism, oh yes, that he has communed with old gods and the forces of nature, but where was his magic when the inquisition came? Where is it now? Just a head-cracked old man who spent too long in Catemaco and lost his sense of reason. I told him it would get him in trouble. A thousand times, I told him, but he said it was history, our history, dammit." He sank his tired head into his hands. "This was meant to be his funeral, now that he's gone for good."

"He survived a month in D'Ulua," the gunman offered. "Maybe his reputation for miracles isn't unfounded."

"Cartegena is different. He's going there to die."

The three men all looked down glumly. The fight left them, and they all appeared to be very much of a type with the maroons we had picked up in Bermuda—battered by a storm to the point of their spirit breaking. They were tired of resisting and tired of fighting. They were ready to give up.

Although these men did not believe that the old Victoria was a sorcerer, I wasn't much deterred by their skepticism. Such men, who identified themselves with the new age of reason, would be the first to reject such things, and to paint supernatural occurrences as simple tricks of the mind. They would reject the existence of Toussaint's curse, if they knew of it, and would reject my sense of the storm's malevolence even if they had stood through it beside me. At the very least, Old Victoria had claimed to know how to commune with gods, and that was what we needed.

"You said that he left for Cartegena today...from D'Ulua?" I asked, breaking the sullen silence. "Are they going by boat?"

"I believe so," Young Victoria said hesitantly. "On an Inquisition vessel. *El Sabueso*."

Toussaint muttered to me, "The same one that was three times our size," pointedly, as he already knew what I was thinking of.

"Every ship is bigger than ours," I said quickly back to him. "That's no excuse."

"It's not just the size," Toussaint said. "An inquisition ship... they are well-armed, but more than that, they are fanatics: not the type to make an easy surrender."

"I'm hearing that it will be dangerous."

"It is too dangerous to attempt. People will be hurt."

"Let's ask the crew. Maybe they will surprise you. If they want to be there to help, you ought to let them."

Toussaint ran an anxious hand through his hair, looking torn. "I don't want...this is the most selfish thing I could ever ask. Some of them don't even believe in the curse. The captain doesn't believe me. Why should I ask him to endanger his life for such a thing?"

The other three men watched us bicker with narrow eyes and scheming mouths.

"Not only mercenaries, then," Victoria said.

"Mercenaries too." Toussaint shrugged, and cheekily added, "Available for hire, as it happens, and a bounty may go a long way towards convincing our crew to hop on a fool's mission."

The other two men looked to Victoria. The haunted man dangled his father's medallion in front of him again, and watched it in thought.

"Goddamn the fool son of a foolish father," he cursed. "But what else is there to lose?"

We hurried back to port, with our weapons restored to us and a five pound-sterling down payment for a new mission: the recovery of Old Juliano Victoria from the recently departed Inquisition ship. I jittered in excitement all the way down, and kept pulling ahead of Toussaint by long strides. Indecision slowed him down, as much as excitement sped me up.

"I won't be convincing them," Toussaint warned me. "I would not feel right about doing so."

The crew, as a collective, was still awake when we arrived back at the *Villainelle*, though surly and sober, rationing out among themselves what little alcohol they had managed to sequester away from the inquisition. They were trapped on the boat this evening, and all they had to entertain themselves with was laying about and talking, and several were already gone to sleep. They received Toussaint's reappearance with pleased surprise.

I raised my voice, told them of our plan, and the (admittedly meager) reward that awaited us upon its completion. I did not mention that Victoria was a sorcerer, nor that we had a personal reason for pursuing him. I didn't need to. The others were restless, and had been spending the past few hours griping about the Spanish and the Inquisition. After the measly reward we'd earned for coming all this way, and the poor reception and robbery we'd suffered under their watch, they were itching for a bit of vengeance against the Inquisition. Zayne was so vocally in support of launching an attack against them that his crewmates had to repeatedly pull him down and quiet him and remind him that the fort across the harbor still had its cannons pointed in our direction. The vote to follow *El Sabueso* passed quickly, and we began readying ourselves for departure by moonlight.

Eight for Defeat

We were roughly six hours behind the Inquisition ship by the time that we cast off from Vera Cruz. We knew their destination—Cartagena—so we knew they were likely to hug the coast until they passed around the Yucatan and down to Columbia. We were moving faster than they were, but it wasn't until well after noon that we spied *El Sabueso* on the horizon.

"Is that them?" Toussaint asked.

"They're flying the Standard," Socks said, clapping his spyglass shut. He gave the order: pass them by to the north. We would pull out of their sight range and hurry ahead to the northernmost point of the Yucatan Peninsula. There, we would lie in wait among the mangroves to ambush the other ship when the peninsula forced them northwards.

It was a simple enough thing to sail ahead of *El Sabueso*. Our light vessel was still faster than any other ship in the world, and especially faster than a heavy Inquisition gunship. With the northern winds behind us, we flanked them long, long before they reached the tip of the Yucatan. Socks directed us to continue ahead for another hour further, trying to time when the inquisition would pass by our hiding place so that it would be as close as possible to sunset. Then we nestled ourselves up in the shoreline and waited.

For more than an hour, we waited: tense and poised to spring. There was an air of anxiety about today's preparation. Everyone knew that our opponent was not going to be another helpless merchant vessel. They were neither cowardly nor weak. Even in the best of circumstances, we were going to come out of this fight with some injuries.

I was armed with two pistols, tucked into the holsters of a bandoleer that slung loosely over my shoulder, as well as my uncle's cutlass on my hip. Our pistols were loaded with one shot each, and it was custom to carry multiple guns rather than waste time reloading. Sometimes a fight would be won or lost in the time it took to reload a single weapon, so it was better to simply drop one once it was spent and draw out a new one. Jaks carried six pistols on his bandoleer, and the top one bounced up against this chin with the rising and falling of our ship upon the waves.

Toussaint dealt out playing cards as a way to pass the time and distract from the impending battle. He was terrible at cards, and always liable to lose the entire contents of his purse in a night. He kept his table to four at a time, and lost himself a good pile of silver, bit by bit, in hopes of raising the morale of his crew.

When Socks put out the call that the target had finally appeared on the horizon behind us, Toussaint and One-eyed John were finishing out a hand of five-card stud. Toussaint was showing a pair of black sixes and the jack of clubs, while John had a hand of sequential diamonds: jack, queen and king.

"Let us be packing up," Toussaint said cheerfully, but John caught his hand before he could pick up the cards.

"We oughta finish the hand," John protested. "I have a feeling I'm going to like how this goes. We have to wait for them to get out ahead of us, anyway."

Toussaint grimaced, but those others of us who had gathered around to watch or play all agreed: it was bad luck to call off the hand early.

Toussaint dealt John the ace of diamonds, and himself the six of hearts.

John grinned like a demon and said, "All in."

"Fold," Toussaint answered immediately, looking very unhappy, and flipping all of his open cards upside down to show his surrender.

"Haha!" John exclaimed and flipped up his hidden card: a worthless queen of clubs. "I had nothin'," he gloated.

"Well played," Toussaint muttered.

"What'd you have?"

John flipped Toussaint's hand over and spread the cards out, despite Toussaint's tardy attempt to keep them hidden. His last card was the Jack of Spades. He'd held a full house of sixes over jacks: a hand that would have beaten John even if his hidden card had made him a straight or a flush as he had pretended. A pair of black jacks—called 'fish hooks' for how the "J" hooks around—plus the devil's number, 666, added up to a bad omen. It was called by some the devil's hand, devil's line, or, sometimes, the dead man's hand, and it portended an imminent, violent disaster.

A hush fell over the table. Captain Socks was a very practical man who did not give credence to superstition. It was only because of this level-headedness that Toussaint could have a place on a ship here, given his famous reputation for bad luck. Socks tended to attract people who shared his disdain for portents and omens, but even so, there is a limit to what people can reasonably abide. Most sailors would have abandoned the mission immediately upon seeing the devil's hand, and some would have marooned Toussaint just for showing it. Socks' order came across the silence to get up and get ready for the attack, but the crew hesitated.

"Do not worry overmuch," Toussaint said, collecting all the cards so that they would be out of sight. "We are old friends, the devil and I."

"Do you really—?" John started to ask.

"Of course," Toussaint said. "Up, everyone. If we are not ready, they will be out of our reach, and you will call that bad fortune. Up! The devil loves a lay-about; he hates a man who makes him run."

El Sabueso entered our range right before sunset. We waited for them to pass, then shot out from the coast so swiftly that, in a matter of minutes, we were coming up behind them to the west, hiding in the fierce glare of the setting sun. By the time the sun had sunk into the water and blessed us with nighttime, we managed to slip up alongside the taller ship, as slick as a shadow. As we approached, we trimmed our main sail and only used the small forward jib to bring us up against the looming deck of *El Sabueso*. We secured ourselves to their hull with hooks and tethers, while the first boarders scurried up the rigging.

Zayne was up first, with a knife in his teeth. The first guard was coming over to investigate the sounds of tapping on the hull when Zayne's fingers hit the top of the railing.

"Huh?" was all the guard said, as Zayne took his knife and swung with a wide arc through the man's throat. He fell forward, and someone else caught his body on our deck below.

Zayne ran up behind the second guard and got him with another knife across the throat. He made a gurgling noise as Zayne lowered him to the ground. The last guard looked around at the noise, but a bolt from Stache's crossbow took him in the ear and sent him toppling over the side into the sea.

At least. That was how we planned it to go: quick, deadly, and one-sided. But we ran into a bit of bad luck.

The sun had just set, and we were lowering our main sails, coming up behind the Inquisition ship, when one of our pistols went off. A misfire: a crack that echoed across the water as clear as a bolt of lightning on a clear night. I held my breath, as if that silence would right the mistake. We all froze together in one long moment of indecision, then a warning bell rang out on *El Sabueso*, and lantern lights flashed on one after another.

"Forward! Secure the mainsail, top speed," Toussaint bellowed from the helm, his voice a slap to jolt us awake. "Boarders to the grappling lines!"

With many curses, the crew jumped to our positions. We were closing quickly on the *El Sabueso*, but their deck soon populated itself with inquisition sailors and soldiers, all scurrying around each other like a bunch of angry hornets around a kicked nest. Fresh ripples ran across their sails as they started on a banking turn, intending to bring their stinging cannons around to face us.

I seized onto my grappling line—a long rope suspended from the top of the mast—amid my fellow crewmates as we raced closer. I stared at the cannons with wide eyes, helplessly twisting the coarse hempen rope in my hands. They spun closer and closer. Then we slammed our forward ram into the other ship. We speared it up upon our great horn with a force that raised half its hull out of the water.

I jumped with the impact, and it carried me forward on my swinging rope. Our deck disappeared from underneath me, and I flew out over the sea. My feet kicked out ahead of me and caught themselves up on the railing of *El Sabueso*. While the inquisition crew were down on their hands and knees, still knocked off balance from the force of the ramming, the *Villainelle* pirates swarmed over them. Some of us launched further onto the deck, into the midst of the stumbling inquisitors, while others landed low against the hull and had to grapple with rigging to bring themselves topside. They went running up to do battle, while I teetered on the edge.

A leather-faced sailor on his knees put his hand to the railing beside me. He was outfitted for sleep, not battle, and had only a light shirt as cover. I drew my cutlass. The sun had drawn lines on this man's face much deeper than someone his age should have, especially down around his mouth. He looked tired—and scared—but I was afraid as well, and my sword was already swinging down when he turned his fear back up at me.

A pirate at last. A murderer at last. I was not prepared in my mind for the moment, which struck me with nausea.

When I dropped from the railing onto the deck proper, a wild-eyed man wearing the uniform of an inquisition soldier came running at me with his blade drawn. I blocked his swing with my bloody sword, and the impact sent flecks of blood flying onto my face and clothes. He seemed surprised that I had met his strike. His momentum carried us together into the railing, where he forced our two interlocked swords down into me. He pressed his blade down through the leather on my shoulder into my skin while I fumbled with my other hand through my bandoleer. His breath smelled of alcohol, and his spittle flew onto my face as he said some Spanish insult that was lost in the ringing of battle.

My fumbling fingers found the bone-smooth handle of my pistol. I turned the tip towards his gut and pulled the trigger. The bullet shattered the bone in his hip and sent him sprawling onto the deck with a scream. I plunged the tip of my sword into his chest, and he was quiet.

I sat back against the railing, feeling woozy, and pushed over the first man's body so that he would stop staring at me. One-eyed John opened the door to the lower deck and caught a cloud of gun-smoke in his face, as two muskets fired off at him at once. Zayne leapt over his body into the smoke with a holler, disappearing below deck and making those beyond yell out in terror. Jaks ran after Zayne, shouting back a curse and a command to follow.

As I stood, the bandoleer fell from my shoulder; the inquisitor's sword had severed its strap. I realized that the blood soaking through my shirt was my own, and clamped a hand onto my shoulder in an attempt to squeeze my wound shut. I pulled out my remaining pistol from the fallen leather spool and stuck it into my belt before following Jaks below deck.

The inside of the ship was dark and muffled. The sounds of battle were at once all around me and nowhere at all. I stepped past two fallen Spanish soldiers, who had great gashes cut across their bodies but still writhed around on the ground in the slow process of dying. I continued forward through the corridor, following the sound of clashing steel, until I came across Zayne and Jaks.

Zayne was slipping down against a wall, struggling to stay on his feet while blood gushed from a hole in his head where his ear used to be. Jaks stood between him and the enemy, weaponless, with the last of his spent pistols smoking in his hand, and his one cutlass knocked to the floor. Blood bloomed through his shirt from several small stab wounds on his chest and arms. As I pulled up behind him, Jaks gave a final curse and fell over.

An inquisition nobleman barred the stairwell down to the lowest deck. He wore a well-waxed mustache and appeared uninjured, if a little winded. He bore a light, chain-armored cuirass, and flourished his fancy silver rapier with a flick that flung blood down from the tip. He carried himself like a trained swordsman.

"An African, a mut, and now a little girl," the man said with a smirk.

"Get back, Mouse," Zayne grunted at me, as he pushed himself up. He raised a sword in one hand, while the other steadied himself on the wall, but he had not the strength to lift it up above his elbow.

I drew my gun and pointed it at the duelist, although, because of the wound in my shoulder, I could not lift it very high either. "Drop your sword," I commanded. "Or I will kill you."

The inquisitor held his arms out to the side and lifted his face up towards the ceiling. He closed his eyes and quoted: "'Behold, I have given you authority to tread on serpents and scorpions, and over all the power of the enemy, and nothing shall hurt you.'"

I pulled the trigger, and the empty click of a failed mechanism betrayed us all. Divine misfortune—it did not fire.

The inquisitor twisted his neck to the side with a wolf-like smile, then leapt at me with his rapier.

Zayne intercepted. With a roar, he shoved off from the wall and launched himself into the charging man. The inquisitor twisted, blocking with his sword on instinct. The thin blade cut into Zayne at the shoulder, all down his torso, through the leather, but the rapier was a small thing and it did not stop his charge. Zayne hugged the blade between them as he crashed the duelist into the wall on the other side of the corridor.

The inquisitor struggled to push his sword through Zayne's shoulder, to cut him through and push him off, but rapiers are made for stabbing, not bisecting. I snarled, charged, and watched his expression turn from one of confidence to terror. I thrust the point of my cutlass into his face, breaking through teeth and pushing into the back of his throat. The swordsman gurgled and wobbled with my blade stuck in his mouth. Then he fell to the ground.

I caught Zayne as he fell afterwards. By 'caught,' I mean that I directed his fall so that he landed on his back instead of his face. He grunted in pain at the impact, which at least let me know that he was still alive. His leathers had stopped some of the sword's progress into his torso, but it was all dark with blood. Babbling curses, I tried in vain to hold the whole of his chest together with my two little hands.

"Stache!" I yelled backwards, heedless of who else might hear. "I need help down here! Stache!"

Zayne didn't say anything. He smiled at me, as if I were the one in need of comfort. He held a hand up to my chin, and cupped it, and left a bloody smear on my cheek where he drew his thumb across it.

I ripped a cloth from my shirt and held it against his head wound until help arrived. I don't know how long it was. He was still alive when Stache came and ripped open his tunic, to pour alcohol on his wound. Zayne screamed and cursed in hallucinatory Spanish, yelling at the devil to wait to set him afire until he got to hell. Stache gave me a bottle of some tonic and told me to force him to drink it. I did so numbly—he was too weak to resist—and soon the sedative sunk him to sleep.

"Is he going to be okay?" I asked the taciturn sawbones.

Stache shook his head but didn't say anything else, as he worked quickly to sew the chest wound together with jagged, rough stitches. It wouldn't stop bleeding.

This was a mistake, I thought, as I stared down at Zayne's body. This whole venture was a mistake. It would not be worth it if this man died because of me. Yet there was nothing I could do, except pray, and there was no god to whom I might pray anymore. I was a cursed woman, hooked on the devil's line.

Then, with a shock, I realized that there was someone else to whom I could go for help.

I leapt up suddenly. Stache paid me little mind—so focused was he on his work—as I ran down, past the groaning Jaks and the body of the duelist, down stair to the belly of the ship. I ran through the kitchen, which was well stocked with all sorts of hanging herbs as might be necessary to satisfy a noble's appetite, and into the brig.

The brig was dark. Torture instruments hung from the walls, creaking endlessly with the swaying of the ship. One lantern hung from a chain by the room's entrance, and I brought it with me into the darkness. The prisoners of the inquisition were all shoved up in pens, and they clamored at the bars with a desperate need to see what was happening.

"Which of you is Victoria?" I called out to them.

"Who wants to know?" one man answered. He had a long prisoner's smock, a scabbed cut over his eye, and many layers of yellow, blue, and red bruises, all in varying stages of healing. His hair and beard both were long, dark gray, and matted.

I hurried to his pen, bearing a ring of keys that I found hanging from the wall. "Your son sent us," I told him.

"No, he didn't," Victoria said with a sharp-eyed squint. I must have had a familiar look on my face, for he continued, "You need a miracle."

"Aye, more than one," I answered, as I tried the keys on the ring one by one. My fingers shook and fumbled, and I kept knocking the keys by accident into the metal beside the lock. "I have friends who are injured. Do you have a spell for fixing wounds?"

"Si, a miracle for a miracle; I am in your debt already." He held his right hand out through the bars for a handshake. It was missing all of its fingernails.

A key finally turned in the lock, and I opened up the cage. I didn't shake the man's hand, but as he marveled at the sweet novelty of freedom, I took him by the forearm, and pulled him along with me, back through the kitchen.

Following the old man up the stairs was agony, as he had to take each step with first one foot, then the other, before moving on to the next one. Even if he was healthy before, a month of incarceration and torture had left his knees too rusty to bend. He stepped on the body of the dead nobleman rather than over it, then knelt down with a loud groan between Jaks and Zayne. Stache had already moved on, back upstairs, in response to another call for help; he couldn't do much more for the two injured men, and it hadn't taken him long to do everything he could. Both of them were still alive, but unconscious, and bleeding through their hastily applied bandages.

Old Victoria peaked under the bandages, frowned, then forced himself back up to his feet.

"Going back down," he grunted to me. "Come; I'll need your knees."

"But there's nothing down there, is there?" I asked.

"There's enough," he said. "There are barrels of water in the kitchen. Bring one up, if you can."

I ran ahead of Victoria, down to the kitchen, where I found a cook cowering behind a table. The cook jumped up and yelled at me in some very rapid Spanish that he surrendered, and begged me to let him live. I told him I would give him this mercy, if he helped me carry a water barrel. Even with the two of us, the barrels were too heavy to lift. I abandoned the full ones, taking instead a barrel that was already spouted and had most of its water spent. It would have to be enough.

Meanwhile, Victoria gathered herbs from the kitchen. He had a mortar and pestle which he used to make a fine orange-red powder of dried peppers. As I stumbled underneath the barrel, my wounded arm hurt like it was getting ripped off of my torso. He came up and rubbed some of the powder into the gash on my shoulder. It stung like my arm was caught aflame. I cursed, my vision blurring from the pain.

"It stops bleeding," Victoria explained, and directed me to look at my wounded shoulder, which in fact had continued to bleed since I received it, and was now soaking in the powder. It looked like the powder was drying out the wound, which I didn't think could be right.

"I'd appreciate a warning," I muttered, feeling nauseated.

"Use the rest on those wounded men up there," Victoria commanded, pouring the rest of the red powder into a handkerchief which he stuck in my pocket. "Give them water, and drink some yourself, if you want to keep your senses about you." Victoria then went back to gather rosemary, sage, and thyme from the herbal offerings of the kitchen, which he ground into a poultice. Bless the Inquisitor's taste for flavorful dishes, that he carried so many herbs with him.

Zayne's head wound was bleeding the worst. I sprinkled the pepper powder into it, and he mumbled another incoherent curse about fire and the devil, but he was too weak to do anything but shake his head around a little. I sprinkled a little of powder into each of their wounds—Zayne's first and Jaks' second—but wasn't confident that it would be enough.

When Victoria arrived with his herbal poultice, he handed me some lemons and instructed me to squeeze juice into cups of water for them to drink. While I administered water, he washed the wounds, applied his poultice, and then used clean rags from the kitchen to dress them.

"Are you really a sorcerer?" I asked him once I ran out of water and energy at once. I sat with my back against the bulkhead, dizzy from blood loss. "Or just a physic?"

"A shaman," he responded, with his hands busy at work.

"You aren't saying any magic words."

"No point, if they can't hear me," he said. "Sometimes 'you're going to be okay' can work magic enough."

"That's not magic."

"Judge for yourself once they awaken," he said. "You can't understand it? It's magic. I understand it: I'm a magician."

"But can you talk to gods?"

"Anyone can talk to gods. It is getting them to listen that is the tricky part."

"But can you?"

"That's your second miracle?" he asked, squinting at me from the corner of his eye. "Yes, I know a ritual, but to journey to the realms of gods is not without its dangers."

I collapsed back against the bulkhead, flushed with relief that there was a point to this bloodshed after all. I hadn't realized before that moment how much my faith had taxed me, knowing (without allowing myself to think it) that all of this might have been in vain.

"Thank god," I said to myself.

"Which one?" Victoria answered wryly.

The battle was over, and we won the day, but it was not without its costs. We had a great number of injured men on our side, and although Jaks and Zayne survived their wounds, the latter would have a nasty scar now in place of his ear. John was dead. He had taken two musket balls to his chest, and died where he fell. I am told that, with his last words, he cursed the dead man's hand.

Once we'd thoroughly pillaged *El Sabueso*, taking its rich foods and wine, gold and gunpowder, we set the rest of it aflame. We took the inquisition's prisoners with us, not wanting to condemn them to the fire, and planned to release them on the continent where next we landed. I met with Toussaint on the deck later. He pretended to be satisfied with the outcome while we turned the ship around to the west and headed for Catemaco: the secret city of sorcerers.

Nine for Heaven

Monkeys hooted at our ship from the branches of mangroves as we rowed our way through the brackish water of the Sontecomapan Lagoon. The mangroves grew so thickly together that their roots hid any rock, sand, or dirt that we might have otherwise seen on the shore, encasing them in a wooden net of rope-thick roots that stretched out into the water like so many long-fingered hands. This was a good place to become lost in. There was no hint of civilization in this part of the jungle, and the harbor was so shallow that even our light ship found itself scraping against the bottom. On one occasion, we grew so entrenched in mud that the crew had to hop down into the waist-deep water, perch ourselves atop buried mangrove roots, and rock the boat back and forth with coordinated pushes until it finally came free. After that, Socks declared we had gone far enough, and we rowed ourselves back into a deeper inlet to lie low.

Juliano Victoria had directed us to this lagoon because it was only a four-hour hike south from the innermost estuary to reach his home on Lake Catemaco. It appeared to be a safe place for the *Villainelle* to hide, in case the Spanish were to stumble upon the inquisition wreck and raise the alarm for pirates in the area. Toussaint warned me to keep quiet about the real reason why he was going to be hiking deep inland with one of the inquisition's prisoners, so that he could spin some complicated story about it, but I felt sick in my gut with guilt. John was dead, and Zayne was still unconscious with a fever, and all for a cause that they didn't know anything about. My guilt was giving me nightmares of dead men, so I spoke the truth to the captain, and it was not received well.

Toussaint tried to mollify him. "There is no material difference to you whether I had my own reason to chase the ship. The rest of you were eager enough without it to follow after. What is the relevance of my reason to you?"

"It's not a matter of reason," Socks argued. He did not yell—even when raised, his voice was soft—but an uncharacteristic tightness around his mouth and eyes betrayed the wrath beneath them. "It's a matter of principle that the crew ought to be fully informed when we take a vote."

"The extra information is a positive for me, but it is neither positive nor negative for you, so for what purpose ought I have shared it?"

"It is negative, Toussaint! It is nonsense, and you put our lives in danger for it."

They kept arguing around one another without finding common ground until Socks snapped and demanded that Toussaint leave the ship. He could take the pinnace, and his sorcerer as well, if he really wanted to, but he shouldn't be surprised if the *Villainelle* was not here when he returned. The rest of the crew would take a vote whether they would wait for him to finish his nonsensical mission; a vote for which all parties would be fully informed. If not, he would have to look for the ship again himself on the great blue sea.

Toussaint heatedly accepted, taking Victoria into the Pinnace and lowering them both down to the water before I realized that he was trying to leave me behind.

"Do you truly think that I would let you abandon me again?" I said down to him, perching with a foot on the *Villainelle's* railing.

"You do not need to join me in my banishment," Toussaint said without looking up at me. "The fault is with me, he knows. Besides, you are injured."

My arm was in a sling, bandaged around the shoulder, and it hurt like hell when I jumped down the five feet to the pinnace. The boat rocked wildly at the impact, but I caught the mast with my good arm, and hid my pain under bravado.

"You ought to know better," I told him. I would not be heartbroken if the *Villainelle* left me. After the attack on the Inquisition ship, I was not feeling so proud about being a pirate (*that* kind of pirate, anyway). I was all for the bravado and the taxing of the rich, but the killing and the dying were not really to my taste.

Toussaint laughed and rubbed his brow, caught somewhere between amusement and consternation. "I ought to," he agreed. "My apologies: loneliness is not an easy habit to forget."

We took the pinnace down through the winding marsh, pushing southward. Toussaint took the till. He put a hand on my shoulder, in apology, and his touch gave me goosebumps, oh very familiar goosebumps. I put my hand over his. In these touches, we had a wordless conversation, where he apologized for wrapping me up in his troubles, and I assured him it was my choice and I did not blame him for it. It was a conversation that we'd had before, so words were not necessary.

When the trees grew too thick for us to traverse farther into the lagoon, we tied up our boat to a mangrove root and made the rest of the way on foot. Victoria assured us that Lake Catemaco was massive, and we would certainly come across it eventually so long as we continued to follow Toussaint's compass southward, but it was a long and exhausting hike through the jungle to get there. The air was cloying, and we were incessantly beset by mosquitoes. Busy as I already was batting away melancholic thoughts (of John and Zayne and the men I'd killed with my own hands), I quickly grew irritable at the insects' biting, and not at all in the mood for conversation. Toussaint, however, was not one to abide silence.

"Victoria," he said lightly as he lifted a low-hanging branch for the old man to pass underneath. "Tell me; how is it that you became a sorcerer? It is not a common vocation, even in these parts of the world, or is it indeed?"

Juliano Victoria was a tall, brown man who hunched over as he walked, and only ambled along at a speed that made our tour through the jungle take twice as long as it would have if Toussaint and I were traveling alone. His brow drooped heavily over his eyes, giving him the appearance of sleepwalking even when waking.

"It's my ancestral way," he said, his voice labored from the effort of the hike. "I studied with magicians of the mind in Germany, and with Irish occultists, but Catemaco gave me the sorcerer's name."

Toussaint pressured Victoria to tell us about his history as we walked. His father had been a plantation owner in Vera Cruz, who married an indigenous woman, and, according to Juliano, that's the last decent thing his father ever did. Victoria escaped to Europe as soon as he was able, in order to chase an obsession with the supernatural, but then he returned when his parents died. He committed himself to honoring the memory of his mother and her culture rather than that of his father. He spent decades collecting the histories and artifacts of empires and peoples which were here first. Sorcery was only a small part of it, but it was what he became known for.

Victoria stopped and pulled us aside towards the trunk of an old tree, which was moss-covered and wreathed in vines. Some of these vines were loose and looping, but one was so tightly twisted around itself that, like an overspun rope, it knotted in and truncated its own length with knobby protrusions. He instructed us to cut out as much of the vine as we could carry.

"What is this?" Toussaint asked, as he used his cutlass to saw through the thick, fibrous material.

"It is the beanstalk to the giant's cloud," was the sorcerer's cryptic answer.

Toussaint treated the vine with much more reverence as he made the second cut, carving out a section as long as the distance from his hip to the ground. It was heavier even than a log of the same size would be, and he struggled to hoist it across his shoulders.

"So you do know of this way already, to speak with the god?" Toussaint grunted, with the vine-yoke in place. "Have you spoken with him before?"

"Only to his brethren," Victoria said.

The sorcerer's voice was still hoarse from captivity, and it seemed to hurt him to say much. Or maybe he was only secretive. Toussaint pressed him for more details, but it was in his sorcerous nature to be elusive. He said that he was only there to broker a conversation between us and our god, not to give away knowledge that we had not earned.

"Tell me your history instead," Victoria huffed. "Let an old man catch his breath."

Toussaint obliged. He told Victoria about how he was sacrificed to Tlaloc as a child, but escaped from that fate, and now was hunted by the god who wanted to collect his due. He left off the details of his gender, which I thought might be relevant, but he seemed not to think so. Something in the story seemed to bring Victoria some distaste, but before that distaste was spoken to, we arrived at the lake.

Lake Catemaco was misted over when we arrived, carrying a gray cloud that drifted up from the water in wisps of steam. Great, swelling trees took up every inch of the coastline, their canopies billowing out from the lake's edge. They were even wilder here than the mangroves of the lagoon had been. As we continued westward along the lake, we spotted the first evidence of humanity: the occasional fisherman's boat, sitting by the warm spotlights between the shadows of leaves where bugs and fish gathered. The Catemaco fishermen must have built their homes up the coast, somewhere within the leaves, as only their docks could be seen jutting out into the water.

In the distance, we spied the few thatched yurts that made up Catemaco's town square, but as we did, Victoria deflected us down a hidden path to his own hut. This path threaded through a small garden, guarded by a pair of sentinel trees, to a small dock with a small boat that sat in algae and moss. The hut was built on stilts in order to protect it from flooding (which was common in this part of the world, with its terribly unpredictable seasons). It was barely large enough for a bed, trunk, and lopsided dresser, all of which showed obvious damage from water and mold. This place would likely not survive another twenty years; the wood was already rotting in places, and everywhere nature encroached upon it with ivy and vines and pushing roots. One of these roots retreated as we stepped upon the hut's damp floorboards, slithering its black body down under the bed.

"Do not harm it," Victoria warned, and he lowered himself gingerly onto his mattress. "Serpents are holy to water gods." He coughed. "That's the hardest that walk has ever been. Give me a moment." He kept coughing, no matter how long he lay there.

I sat on the dresser, scratching at the bug bites on my arms. "Is there anything that we can do while you lay there? To help or prepare?" I struggled to keep my impatience out of my voice.

Victoria sent Toussaint into town and told him to buy two medallions of green jade, each no larger than a piece-of-eight coin. Me, he sent into his garden to gather Mexican marigolds, with their long stems intact. The flowering bush appeared to be a weed, outgrowing and bullying its neighbors in the sorcerer's untended garden plot, but as it had the only yellow flower in sight, I brought back a few samples. It was not enough, and he sent me out again for a good bushel.

The sorcerer then instructed me to use a wooden spoon to skin the bark off of the big vine that Toussaint had brought. It was a very frustrating process, as I only had one arm to work with, and I had to sit on part of the vine to keep it still, and even then it would roll around and make half of my scrapes pointless.

Meanwhile, Victoria sat cross-legged atop his bed and wove the marigold stems together, as a child might make jewelry from wildflowers. When I asked what the marigolds were for, he responded, "They are holy to Tlaloc. These talismans will keep you safe in his realm."

"Is it so dangerous there?" I asked.

Victoria spoke more freely now that we were seated in his home, with his attention on his weaving hands, which worked well enough even without their fingernails. "You will journey to Tlalocan through Apan: the connecting ocean, which unites all great seas, rivers, and lakes. There you may find gods of death, or souls of the drowned. May find his wife—she of the jade skirt—or indeed Tlaloc himself, and that is the most dangerous. He may request that you sacrifice more than you are prepared to give. Indeed, the insult that your friend has paid him is great, and there might be nothing he can offer in contrition but his life."

"What insult?" I asked, unaware of anything that Toussaint had done to the god. He had provoked him in self-defense, but he certainly had no contrition about that.

"Tlaloc was once a great god," Victoria explained, sounding like a governess giving a history lecture. "In Tenochtitlan, his high priest was matched in status only by that of Huitzilopochtli. The livelihood of the empire depended on good weather, and Tlaloc is unpredictable, so the Aztecs offered him human sacrifice twice a year in order to attract his one good face rather than his four disastrous ones. I imagine that such a being would find it difficult to forgive someone who was promised as his first human sacrifice in a hundred years and then fled from that duty."

"But Toussaint wasn't the one to promise a sacrifice," I objected. "He was a victim, not the perpetrator."

"If that was how Tlaloc saw it, then he wouldn't be chasing your friend all these years, would he?" Victoria shook his head. "To the Aztecs, sacrifice was a display of respect. They believed that the world only exists through an enduring sacrifice of the gods—if Tlaloc never gave of himself to bring the rains, then the world would die—so to give of ourselves back to him is expected and natural. A pious Aztec would never act as your friend has."

I bit my tongue to keep from arguing with the sorcerer. It wasn't him I had a problem with; he was only telling me the history. When Toussaint returned, he took over for the skinning of the vine, and then once it was skinned, he and I took turns pounding the pale core fibers down with a wooden mallet until they were flat. The process was long and boring, and the sun was low in the sky by the time we were finished. Victoria then set the flattened vine to stewing out over a fire pit in his garden and told us to get some sleep. The last ingredient had to be picked at sunrise, and we would need all of our strength for the ritual.

Toussaint and I slept next to one another on the sorcerer's mildewed mattress. I had a terrible uneasiness, watching him drool in his sleep, that this was going to go terribly wrong. What could we offer to a god? What did we matter to a god, beyond the perceived insult? I watched him nervously. I wanted to keep him safe.

We arose in the navy darkness before the sun.

Victoria kept the shrub in his garden. Choked as it was with weeds, the shrub was twisted but still alive, and the sorcerer commanded us each to pluck the lowest leaf, with a prayer to the gods for gratitude.

"Thank the oneness for these keys to the hidden ocean, and promise to tread respectfully."

The stewing potion was by now the color of raw clay—reddish brown—and after Victoria had ground up and added the shrub leaves, its steam darkened, and something in the smell changed so that it stuck to the back of my throat. It was a dirty, grassy smell, like sod after rain. Victoria hoarsely chanted in some strange language as he stirred the concoction. Finally, he ladled out a serving of potion to each of us, in a pair of cups just slightly more clay-brown than the liquid that filled them.

"Drink," he commanded. "All of it."

It was painful to keep down, like a muddy whiskey which warmed me up all the way from my mouth to my stomach. I held a fist to my neck, struggling to keep it all inside, until Victoria came to fasten his completed talisman around my throat. The woven stems of marigold made a skinny green rope, with the occasional flower adorning it as a jewel, and nestled in the center were the jade disks that Toussaint had found in town. Victoria tied a talisman around each of our throats and instructed us to follow him.

"While we walk," Victoria said, "I want you to focus your mind's eye on that warm feeling in your stomach. Hold on to it like a precious egg. Place both hands on your belly like so, and cradle that egg down to the dock."

"Why the dock?" I asked.

"What did I say about questioning? Don't; just follow."

I began to feel strangely wavy as we laid down on the dock, with our heads lowered over the edge just far enough that our eyes sank under the surface of the lake. The water felt like a breeze, no wetter than the air that held the rest of me. I opened my eyes underwater for a moment and saw the water as a swirling vortex of otherworldly colors, but I was unprepared to see it, and the sight stung my eyes, so I closed them again.

I was vaguely aware of Victoria chanting to us from back on the dock, but his words lost their meaning somewhere between his mouth and my ears. I only experienced the images that the words evoked in my mind's eye, and the feeling of warmth that spread steadily across my body. This warmth began with the potion in my stomach, and everywhere it spread went numb, feeling nothing but melting weakness.

I saw myself standing atop a great, sunken stairwell, with the bottom as dark as the deepest depths of the sea. I saw myself walking down, slowly, one step at a time, and with each step I felt my body relaxing. My feet met water on the third step, and I felt the warmth of it squish between my toes. A numbing feeling crawled up my legs, and the tiny hairs on my legs floated and tickled and then went limp. I walked down slowly, lazily, into the water—a fourth, fifth, sixth, seventh step. The warmth of the water matched and mingled with the warmth of the potion, swirling around each other inside of me and around me. The magic heat flowed up and down through the veins in my arms; the red and warm and wet rivers inside me carried relaxing magic under my skin and around my bones. When the water lapped up against my lips, I tasted salt and iron and earth in it. I took another step and came under the water completely.

When I opened my eyes, I was suspended in Apan, the great uniting sea, with nothing but endless green water in all directions. A vortex swirled below me, and I allowed myself to sink down into it. The portal opened up and pulled me deeper. I spun about myself, weightless, and heaven and earth traded placed a dozen times before finally I burst through the surface.

Toussaint surfaced beside me, gasping for air, and dripping green water from his hair.

"What, where are we?" he babbled.

"Tlalocan," I answered.

The sky overhead appeared green rather than blue, and it tinted the whole of this other reality with an alien verdancy. The sea was a darker shade of green than the sky, dotted with dark-brown islands made not of dirt or sand, but of the twisting together of wet wood. These were the roots of mangroves, which had been so eager to outgrow the land above ground that they pushed their way out of our world entirely and down, down into the depths of the all-connecting ocean. Here, these forking tendrils clawed out of the water and clamored upside down around one another, twisting themselves into knotted landmasses. They sunk themselves into the ruins of sunken ships and drowned stone structures, burying them in gnarled cocoons. I looked around for signs of movement or life, but the place was quiet and cold.

"Do you hear that?" Toussaint asked me. "I think that someone is crying."

As he drew attention to it, the sound came to my ear. A woman's sobbing, which sounded like it was coming from one of the larger mangrove islands, which had streams of water pouring off of it like rivers to feed the great sea.

In this place, like in a dream, to think of moving was the same as moving, and as soon as we thought of swimming towards the source of the sound, we were there at the edge of the island, climbing up the slimy roots. In another instant, we stood atop them, and then in another, we were pushing our way upriver through the twisted trunks of pseudo-trees, in pursuit of the siren's cries. The wood was all damp and slimy, like after a long period of rain, but it moved aside as easily as if it were made of velvet. I drifted along after Toussaint as he forced his way deeper and deeper inland, and the cries became louder and louder.

The central ruin—around which all of this island had grown—was an ancient pyramid, made of many stacked stone steps, almost so swallowed by roots as to disappear entirely. Rivers ran down from the central chamber at the top of the pyramid, flowing down the stairs that ran up the center of all four sides. Toussaint climbed without climbing, and I followed, as he burst into the summit chamber.

A woman wept from the central dais, and it was her tears that became the streams that flowed down the pyramid and became rivers to feed Apan. She wept with her head sunk behind her long, tangled green hair. Her skin was sallow, and her green skirt threadbare. She did not notice us enter, but then Toussaint approached her.

"Excuse-moi," he said, "Do I know you?"

The woman gasped at him with a hand drawn across her chest. Her face was long and gaunt, and tears fountained from beneath her big, red eyes.

"Child," she said, her voice flat. She spoke with many combined voices of different languages at the same time. I heard 'child' at the same time as 'enfant' and 'peque' and 'criança' and others I didn't recognize, all layered over one another.

The woman-spirit gestured up to the dais behind her, to a stone basin filled with water, as big as one might take a bath in. I stepped up to look, and gasped as my gaze broke its stone lip, for at the bottom of the basin lay the motionless body of a baby. Toussaint tried to comfort the woman, out of my gaze, and I only heard him vaguely, struck as I was looking upon the drowned child. I couldn't help but reach for it, out of some vain need to save or comfort it, and as my fingers breached the surface of the water, the baby stirred. His mouth opened, and bubbles escaped his lips. He looked at me, and raised his hands, as if in supplication.

Then the weeping woman was there. She shoved me out of the way and pushed her own hands into the water. She squeezed the baby about his neck, and shook him, pushed him into the bottom of the basin, wailing all the while.

I seized the woman from behind, with the thought of moving her, but she was as solid as a monster should be. Her head swiveled to meet me, and her eyes widened.

"So pretty," she said, with echoes of 'bello' and 'jolie' beneath.

Toussaint shouted, "Do not lay a hand…" but the woman's was already grasping my neck. She petted my jade talisman with her thumb, and muttered, "Tlaloc," and "Chaac," and other names for the same being.

I grabbed the lady's wrist. Her fingernails were long, yellow, and jagged as talons. "Yes, where is he, and how will I find him?"

"He will find you now," she said, and squeezed my talisman. She was so strong that to stop her was as impossible as to stop a river with my bare hands, as she took the talisman and ripped it wholly from my throat. She cackled, gleefully, and dove with it into her own tear-stream, disappearing under the surface as if it were a league deep and not only a few inches.

In the distance, thunder rumbled. The stone quivered all around us and the dust of a century fell down on our heads.

"Mariah, hide yourself," Toussaint took my shoulders, panicking. "Leave, go home, get far from here."

"I don't know how."

We ran for the exit to our pyramid chamber, but before we could reach it, a roiling, many-colored mass of wooden snakes crawled in and around the stone entryway. Their bodies were the brown of tree bark, but their faces were each painted one of red, green, purple, blue, or gold. The snakes dove over and into one another as they crawled across the ceiling and walls of the pyramid's sacrificial chamber. They twisted around like the infinitely intertwined roots of mangroves, and soon they covered every stone surface with their bodies. After them followed the five faces of Tlaloc.

As the god emerged from the undulating mass of snakes, they took the form of a hydra, with five long necks made of slithering snakes, each composed only of those belonging to a single color. Their faces became the shape of Tlaloc's mask, with snake-rings as eyes, and many bared fangs and rattling tails as teeth. Where the mouths opened, clouds blew out, as gray and angry as the worst storm. The red-masked head reared back, hissing, and flames spouted out from between its teeth. It lunged at me.

Toussaint jumped between me and the hydra head with his arms out and braced himself to take the attack; however, as the mask neared him, the red in it turned to green, and the hissing, fire-spitting maw re-arranged itself into a jade grin. The body of the creature broke around us like a wave, the wooden froth rolling around without touching us. The big green mask held itself just in front of Toussaint's face, while the red face resurfaced somewhere on the main body far behind it, sulking.

"*Our defiant runaway*," the green face said pleasantly, the many-layered voice sounding much the same as the spirit woman's had, but deeper and warmer. "*Have you come at last to offer yourself to us?*"

The purple face appeared suddenly from behind the green. "MUST YOU END IT EARLY?" it asked with a wagging purple tongue sprouting out from within its teeth. "A SHAME. WE HAVE SO ENJOYED OUR GAME."

"I have come to parlay with you," Toussaint answered. "I mean to find peace."

"Peace is not our way," the gold face said quietly from the background.

"We can hunt longer than you can run, mortal," grumbled the blue face. "You must see that by now."

"But you can see how this circumstance is...not what I would wish," Toussaint said to the monster, with sweat running down from his temple. "And for you as well. I know there is more that you want in this world than just one man such as myself. I am a little thing, but I have abilities that can be utilized to procure any number of treasures greater than myself, which I will gladly pass on to you. Only tell me what you wish, and I will work to make it right. Surely, there is more that I can give to you than my own petty life."

"**You are ours**," the red face hissed, flying in at Toussaint with flames in his mouth and cinders leaping forward, but just as it was about to reach us, the red turned to green, and the mouth parted around us harmlessly, only spraying us with a gentle rainfall.

The red mask reappeared behind us, very put out, with steam dripping from between its teeth instead of cinders. It huffed with a billowing breath, shifting the cloudy mist, and said, "**As the deer belongs to the hunter, you are ours.**"

Toussaint protested, "But I could get you more! Whatever you want."

Purple-mask shimmied to the front, "WHAT WE WANT IS TO CATCH YOU."

"To punish you."

"**To make you suffer.**"

I put a hand on Toussaint's shoulder, and said, "That's not all you want, I know it isn't. You used to have all sorts of sacrifices. You were once honored, and given—"

"*Him.*" Red-mask spat. "**We were given *him*.**"

"We could give you more," I said. "Sacrifice more. Like you had before."

"BUT IS THIS HOW WE REALLY WANT TO END OUR DANCE?" Purple-mask pushed in. "HOW ABOUT A NEW GAME? DEATH OF THE PRECIOUS. SOMETHING PRECIOUS TO US BOTH."

"The death of the precious sustains us," whispered the Gold.

Purple-mask grinned. "WE WOULD HAVE YOUR MARIGOLD, BAD WEATHER. GIVE IT TO US AND YOU MAY HAVE YOUR FREEDOM."

"That is all you want?" Toussaint asked, and he drew his hand to the talisman around his neck. "I am not a fool, Tlaloc. I know that this is what is keeping me safe in your realm. If I were to give it to you, then we would be at your mercy, and forgive me if I do not trust it. I have seen you be ruthless too many times before."

"NO, NOT THAT MARIGOLD," Purple-mask cackled. "THE ONE BEHIND YOU."

"Mary-ah of the Golden Leaf," said gold-mask, the quietest of the five. "Give her to us." It snuck up behind me, and was wrapping me up in snakes before I knew what was happening.

"No," Toussaint answered, frantically pulling off the gold-faced snakes from me. As he touched them, their faces turned green and fled

157

peacefully back to the mass. "This is not possible, not even a decision. She is not mine to give. Nor was I my fathers to give. What is this 'sacrifice' if you can give up that which does not belong to you?"

"That is the offer."

"Refuse it, and we can continue our hunt."

"*Your blood has enjoyed my blessing for twenty years.*"

"You can take your blessings all back! I never wanted them, I never benefitted--."

"*Can you take back a rain after it's fallen?*" Tlaloc asked, all five masks coming together and weaving around each other in a united dance. "**This insult demands blood. You will sacrifice,** to atone for your sin, OR YOU WILL BE HUNTED."

"What sin?" Toussaint asked heatedly. "My birth?"

"It was his father who sinned," I said. "Go send your storms at him."

Green-mask shook its head, "*The one who gave him to us continues to honor us with sacrifice, twice a year.*"

"**You are the only rat to wiggle out of your promise.**"

"My father," Toussaint gasped. "This whole time..."

"**You are a sinner,**" Tlaloc said, and as he spoke he closed his body in around us. The room darkened, and we were forced up against the dais in the middle of the room. "**You are a murderer.** YOU ARE A THIEF. You are a liar."

"A man may be a galaxy..." Toussaint began, but faltered.

"*You look away from the destruction you cause, but it does not disappear,*" said Tlaloc. "*You sow suffering.* **You take and give nothing back.** YOU AND WE ARE THE SAME, BUT WE KNOW WHAT ROLE WE PLAY. *We give of ourself that you may have the lifegiving rains.* **You give nothing.** The world would be better for your death."

I expected Toussaint to bite back with his usual bravado, but he flicked his eyes to me, in a familiar look of pain, then pulled down his hat shamefully over his brow. The monster had cracked him.

"It's wrong," I warned him.

"Look at this moment," he said to me. "If not for me, you would not be here, in this horrible place. You should never be this close to death."

"I am alive," I assured him. "I chose to follow, and you help me how you can."

"I can help you more by dying." He looked so foolishly sullen in that moment that I worried he might actually offer himself up.

I slapped him. The slap amazed and dazed him, and I grabbed him by the shoulders, as he had done to me earlier, and tried to put every fiber of my being into convincing him of what I had to say.

"I would not be better without you. If I had never met you, I would be rotting right now in the bed of a man I hate. I would be living a slow death of sorrow. You showed me how to be brave; no, you saw that I was brave already. You saw through to something good in me that I'd never seen before, and showed me that I could choose a different life. You have been good for me, and I would rather it never rain another day than let you give yourself up."

Toussaint had tears in his eyes, and was beyond speaking, when he embraced me. He kissed me on my lips, and his kiss lit gunpowder in me. I was set afire in an instant, with a blinding white flash that evacuated the moment of everything but us, our lips, and our breath passing hot from his mouth to mine and back. I closed my eyes forgot everything but the feeling of his breath within me. I was desperately in love, with a fury that had me grabbing at the back of his neck and pulling him closer.

When I opened my eyes to see him, we were lying down, side by side, on the dock by Juliano Victoria's home. The old sorcerer was looking away from us, at where his fishing line bobbed in the water nearby.

"I'm sorry," Toussaint whispered to me.

It took me a moment to realize what he meant, and to remember that I wasn't supposed to be in love with him anymore. When the memory returned, I turned to the side, and expelled the clay-orange contents of my stomach into the water. Toussaint looked hurt at that, but then his cheeks puffed out and he did the same on his side of the dock.

"Welcome back to this plane," Victoria said, abandoning his fishing rod. "This is a common reaction; nothing to worry about. Just drink water." He brought us mugs of dirt-speckled water to drink from. They tasted grainy. "Was your journey a fruitful one?"

"Not quite," I said sullenly. "We spoke with them, but they were not, well, agreeable."

Toussaint was still staring down at the lake. His shoulders were tense, and shuddered like he was sobbing. I put a hand on his back.

"Are you here with us?" I asked him.

His eyes darted around like they were chasing fireflies. He did not look sane. He looked as manic as he had been when running around before the god in the middle of a hurricane.

"I know what I need to do," he said, hugging himself around his elbows and rocking back and forth. "And I hate it."

"What is it?" I asked.

"Sacrifice. Blood. Atone. It doesn't need to be my blood; I know whose blood it has to be." He shuddered. "The blood price always should have come from his veins. He paid it with mine, because he could. Because I could do nothing about it. He's kept killing people, twice a year? That's, sacrifice sustains them, that's why they can continue chasing me. Well now I can do something. I can go back and hold a sword to his head and spill his blood all over his evil plantation. It will rain red on the sugarcane of Marie-Galante, and the god will drink his fill."

I was unnerved by his mad conviction. "I don't know that that's the solution. They seemed very much not to want to give you up. It might be for nothing, to go there."

"Or it might be everything. Another game, it wants to play a game with me." Toussaint shuddered. "It is deserved, even if it isn't the answer. It must be done. It's time to do it. Whether it satisfies the god or not, I will serve my father the justice that he deserves."

I laid my arm across Toussaint's shoulders, and embraced him from the side. His skin felt clammy, but his muttering and shivering calmed down as I held him steady. Our communion with the god might not have given us many assurances, but at least it set us on a course with a destination. That course would take us back to Marie-Galante, to confront Toussaint's father and the god together, with our own lives on the line and no magic talismans to protect us. Still, this was far from the first divine confrontation that Toussaint had survived; he recovered quickly, and soon we were on our way.

Ten for Hell

The *Villainelle* left us behind.

Toussaint and I rowed around the Sontecomapan lagoon for half a day, going from one dead end to another, without finding our ship. The mangrove roots felt more menacing to me now than they had when we first landed here, and I jumped at every twitch in the leaves, expecting at any moment for the roots to slither up into our boat and drag us down into Apan. I very much wanted to find our way out of the lagoon sooner rather than later, but Toussaint kept us going around corners, looking for the *Villainelle*.

"I only need to talk to them, to explain, and this will be the last time...he has to know that," He spoke incessantly, out into the water, without needing me to answer. "I didn't know that it was a game. I suppose it was one to me, but now that I know that the demon god thinks it one too, I am going to play to win. You hear me, you heathen bastard of a god? I am going to find my father and I am going to force him to give it all back. I will sacrifice him, it, to you. I'll glut you on his blood. This is your game we play, monster, and I am going to beat you at it." He made quite the picture of madness, calling out into the darkness behind the mangroves, where only monkeys answered.

Eventually, we had to accept the fact of our abandonment and move on. Our heading was to the east—towards the French West Indies from which Toussaint hailed; however, our little one-masted pinnace was little better than a rowboat, and not nearly strong enough to make the journey across the whole breadth of the Caribbean Sea with all of its myriad of dangers. Instead, we made our way along the coastline to Isla Mujeres: a small isle off the east coast of the Yucatan Peninsula, with a very peaceful harbor between island and mainland (making it a popular way-stop for pirates and honest travelers alike). We searched with shaded eyes between the hulls of parked transports for a sign of the low-lying *Villainelle*, but it was not there.

Thus, run out of our other hopes, we sold the pinnace for enough silver to book passage on a ship heading east called the *Argonaute*. It was a slow ship, compared to the *Villainelle*, but much faster than the pinnace and much more likely to survive a storm (and there was always going to be a storm). Once aboard, Toussaint and I stayed apart from the other passengers. We spent our hours resting and writing in notebooks, because our memories of the journey to the other world felt as slippery as dreams, and we intended to record everything we could of our experiences in Tlalocan before the adventure could fade from our minds completely.

At least, that was supposed to be the point of the introspection—that's why Toussaint bought the notebooks in Isla Mujeres—but I found myself quite unable to focus my attention on anything but how the trip ended. The searing light that his kiss brought to the world had given me a feeling of activation. I had felt, in the moment, nothing more than a desire to move forward, to propel into him and do all the human things we were made to do. Did I like it?

Would I like it again? I was beginning to allow myself to think the frightening thought that, despite everything that I knew, the answer might be yes. I stared at him across the deck of the *Argonaute*, where he was bent over his own pen and paper, and imagined what it would feel like to seize him by the coat, throw his paper aside, and wrap him up in a mad embrace. The exercise made me hot in the cheeks with shameful desire.

Before I could collect myself enough to speak of these feelings with him, the *Argonaute* made its first stop: Port Royal. The town looked much the same as when I had first come into port a couple of months ago, albeit with perhaps a little less traffic. I glanced around for the *Triton,* though it couldn't be scheduled to return for another month at least, and of course my uncle would not betray his schedule. I looked anyway, anxious, and ready already to be gone before we ever landed.

Toussaint, on the other hand, wanted to go to shore for a bit.

"They have to come here," Toussaint told me. "We needed repairs after that scuffle with the *Sabueso*. They should have gone to town, and maybe they told someone where they were headed next. The ship could be with a Jamaican shipwright at this very moment, for all we know."

"You can go ashore, but I don't think I should." I didn't want to risk anyone recognizing me as the woman who fled in the night with twenty pounds of the governor's silver.

"Have you looked in a mirror lately?" Toussaint asked me. "You are not the same woman who came to port in August."

It's true. I looked different. My skin was sunburnt and covered in a collection of scrapes and bruises. The saltwater had matted my hair into such a tangle that I had long ago given up on doing anything with it except for bundling the whole mess up. I had thin scabs on the cheek that Jaks had ground into the sand, and although my arm was now out of its sling, I still wore men's clothes, and underneath these, I had discernable muscles quite unlike those which had been there before. I looked weathered. Tough.

Even so, I introduced myself with a fake name wherever Toussaint and I went along the waterfront, trawling taverns for news of the *Villainelle*. We bought ales and sat at the bars and made casual conversation with strangers about who had been by. Toussaint did most of the talking, asking sideways whether there had been anyone interesting in port, or any ships in need of repairs, while I sipped my drink and darted eyes all around the suspicious lot as are likely to frequent a waterfront tavern in the middle of the day.

"Your glare is the scariest thing in this bar," Toussaint said to me over the rim of his tankard, with affection crinkling his eyes.

Despite my intention to pace myself with my drinks, I had become ale-headed, and it tickled me to see his affection.

"Do I scare you, Bad Weather?" I asked, smiling askance.

"Oh very much," Toussaint nodded. "Hell hath no fury like a woman scorned, and you know that I can outrun the dogs of hell, but, aye, I don't think I could shake you if I tried." He took another sip of his drink, looking thoughtful.

"You haven't scorned me," I said.

"Have I not?"

"Not nearly so much as I have scorned you."

Toussaint raised his tankard for a shrug of good-natured chagrin. "'Tis true. I do remember how I bring bile to your lips."

"That was...not you." I looked away from him, into my tankard.

"Aye, aye."

I took a draught for courage, and asked him at last, "Why did you kiss me?"

"Ah, madness," he said evasively, with a poor excuse for a laugh. "Not that it's an uncommon madness with me to want to be kissing someone, but it is not something that I ought to be doing all of a sudden. It shouldn't be a surprise, when it happens, or you get things like that."

"So...why did you?"

He squirmed at being asked the same question again that he'd just avoided. "So this is how you know...it is not my usual choice of engagement, so the why of it...why should one reason with madness? You follow the current, you don't fight against it, and when it drops you off, you're usually still breathing at the least."

I rolled my eyes at him. "Ah, the blatherings of a madman. I assume I should ignore these?"

"If you would be so kind."

"But I..." I lowered my voice. "Have I changed so much that you can mistake me for a man now as well?"

Toussaint was dumbfounded for a moment, then burst out with a laughter of pure bewilderment. I kept looking at him, serious-like, though my embarrassment grew by the second.

"There is," he started, then stopped himself from going down a joking path. "No, that isn't...I am very aware, and you should be too, that you are a woman, and a beautiful woman at that. That...the madness had nothing to do with that, I assure you."

A beautiful woman? I was tumbling over words in my head, smoothing them out, when a dirty man pressed himself up against Toussaint from behind, with a pistol stuck into the back of his neck. A group of his friends encircled us, and their leader hung down an arm about Toussaint's shoulders.

"Imma ask your name, and you answer real careful like," the man said. He was a bristly one, and one of his gray eyes sat dead in its socket. "You Bad Weather? The pirate?"

"Pirate is such an ugly word," Toussaint said, his smile thinning to a razor. "Let me buy you a drink, and we can talk like gentlemen."

"Ain't nothin' gentle about me, pirate," said the grizzly man, who wrinkled his nose with a sharp sniff. "Why don't you stand up real slow, and we'll make a walk of it—"

As soon as they started pulling Toussaint up, and the man training a pistol on him turned it to the side, I slung out one of my pistols towards him. I was as quick as I could be, but one of the other bounty hunters was expecting it. He hit my knuckles with the flat of his blade, sending my gun clattering to the floor.

Having revealed myself to be an enemy, I got my arm yanked roughly back behind my back by another one of the bounty hunters. I cursed as some stitches in my shoulder ripped open and fresh blood soaked into the bandage.

"Foul-mouthed pup," my grabber muttered. I tried to bash his chin with my head, but he was too tall.

Toussaint spoke rapidly. "She's not with me—I only just met her—it's her bad luck to be here, but she seems to have a healthy hatred of you and yours that I daresay I can't find fault with. I don't suppose that's unusual for you, with women."

"Aye, you met her right here?" Grizzly asked. "Then why'd we hear about you going around with some girly from bar to bar, eh?" Toussaint opened his mouth to speak again, but the bounty hunter shoved the nose of his pistol into Toussaint's cheek. "Shush. I ain't listenin' to another word out your mouth but 'yessir', hear me?" He sniffed and jabbed his chin at me. "Take her with us. We're going."

The bounty hunters, true to their word, were not gentle as they dragged us outside and stripped us of our weapons (and our purses, which they deftly pocketed themselves). Though I struggled, the man who held me was skilled in restraint, and my tossing about was ultimately ineffectual. They made mean faces at everyone on the street, scaring them away from interference, and marched us both up the boulevard that led to the governor's mansion.

"Why are we going there?" I asked, as the men pulled up in front of my old fiancé's house. "Aren't we going to prison?"

"Would you rather go to prison?" a man asked wryly, not realizing that, in this case, my answer probably would have been yes.

"Your bounty was set by the governor, direct-like," the leader said. "So we go to him to collect."

The governor's study hadn't changed much since the last time I was there: the same eclectic collection of unorganized books, the same desk and tall window behind it. The only element that was noticeably new was a wanted poster, which the governor had hung up over his treasure chest. The poster advertised that Toussaint 'Bad Weather' Dupuis was wanted alive by the governor of Jamaica for 50 silver pieces. The likeness was remarkably true to life, with Toussaint's billowing hair, tricorne hat, and sharp features. Otherwise, the greatest change was in the governor himself.

Governor Cormorant wore black, even though the heavy clothes made him sweat more than usual. He had lost weight in my absence; his cheeks were unhealthily gaunt, and his eyes had black shadows underneath them. He recognized Toussaint the moment he was duck-walked through the door, and his eyes grew wide with righteous rage.

"We found 'em drinking down by the docks," the bounty hunter leader said, as Governor Cormorant rounded the table, looking nowhere but Toussaint.

Cormorant slapped Toussaint across the face, then seized him by the lapels. "Where is she?" he asked, spit flying from his mouth. Toussaint blinked for a second, in confusion, but in that second, the governor slapped him with his backhand. "Answer me," Cormorant commanded. "What have you done with her?"

Toussaint answered, "If you are speaking of the one I think you are...she should be standing behind me."

Cormorant looked shocked, wrathful, but the slight sliver of hope took his attention off of Toussaint and for the first time turned it onto me. He narrowed his eyes, like it might be a trick, not quite recognizing me, but then those narrow eyes widened bit by bit, until he walked up to me in wonder, hands out, to cup my cheeks and to prove to himself that yes, I was really the same girl that he had loved.

"My dear," he warbled, as his thumb traced the scabs on my cheek. "What has he done to you?"

My jaw dropped, brow furrowed, but before I could answer, Toussaint spoke for me: "Well sir, after I tricked your bride and stole her away in the middle of the night, I decided I ought to make her useful. She's been put to work: scrubbing the decks, and doing womanly things like sewing and the like of which we buccaneers have no skill for."

"Bastard," Cormorant cursed, flying back into his rage. "You dirt-blooded son of a whore." He punched Toussaint in the gut so solidly that I gasped out in sympathy. "To treat my love like some kind of common wench? Get him out of here. To prison! He cannot remain in my presence or I swear by Christ almighty I cannot control my actions. Go!"

"Wait," I spoke up on instinct, without knowing what to say, but Toussaint cut me off.

"Don't," he said, with a sad shake of his head. "Don't pretend. I know you have been counting the days before your beloved could steal you back from me. It will be okay now. You're free now."

I sucked in through my teeth. I was not so quick-witted nor so good a liar as Toussaint, but I was catching up. I realized that this was my fault; I must have done all of this when I signed "Bad Weather" in the governor's ledger. Cormorant had thought, all this time, that I had been kidnapped by a pirate.

"You weren't so bad to me," I said quietly. I yanked backwards on the thick fabric of the governor's coat sleeve and pleaded with him. "Don't hang him."

"Not yet," Cormorant growled. "A hanging is too merciful; I will think on such a punishment as will make hell a relief." Cormorant turned back to me, and his expression changed from rage to cloying affection so quickly that it unsettled my nerves. "My precious darling," he crooned. "You are safe now, and I swear on my life that I won't let that man or anyone else ever hurt you again."

The governor drew me close and petted me on my head, only to pull back his hand and rub his fingers together with disgust at the condition of my hair. Even as Toussaint was being marched out the door, Cormorant was shouting an order out to his staff to draw up a bath for me. I was to be treated with the utmost care and respect, pampered and rejuvenated, and then we would have a banquet at nightfall to celebrate my recovery.

The bath felt unjustly good. I hadn't had the opportunity to properly clean myself—with soap and everything—since I left the governor's mansion. Toussaint had soap on the ship, and he would invite any of the other pirates to scrub themselves down on the deck when it rained (even if he himself waited until the dark dead of the night), but a quick, shy scrub on the deck in my underclothes was nothing compared to a true soak in a tub. It felt like the warmth of the water went so deep that it was softening up my skin and bones both at once.

I had a long time lying there to stew, trying to think about how to turn the strange situation to my advantage, but I had trouble scheming productively. I was exhausted, emotionally, and felt absolutely not up to the task of coming up with a story to spin that would make my host release Toussaint from prison. My friend the pirate was very good at slipping out of these situations by saying the right thing to the right person, but he had clearly left this situation in my hands, and I had no idea what to do. There had to be some solution, some clever combination of words that I could give to Cormorant, but everything that I imagined sounded completely implausible even to me, and the water felt so very nice to doze in.

After I had soaked for so long that my skin was pruning all over, I wrapped myself up in a towel and left the bath chamber for my bedroom. The clothes that I was wearing earlier had all been taken away (perhaps to be incinerated, as they did deserve by that point). A fresh white dress awaited me in its place, as well as a doctor.

The doctor was a skinny, bookish, red-headed Scotsman. I sat on the bed in a towel as he cleaned out my newly re-opened wound and wrapped it up in a fresh bandage. He did not bother to engage in conversation, aside from the barest of instructions. After finishing with the most obvious wound, he moved on to check the rest of me for damage, and, finding nothing that gave him reason to do more than grunt or nod, he informed me he was to check if my virginity was still intact.

"Absolutely not," I said, seizing the man by the wrist as he reached for me.

"You've been in the presence of strange men for months now, and the governor is expecting a virgin..."

"Then he can check that for himself on our wedding night," I said, flushing in the cheeks. I was stronger than the skinny doctor, and threw his hand away from me with an authority that said that I was going to stop him if he tried again.

The doctor frowned. "I will tell him you refused my examination."

"Good," I said, letting my rage and disgust show. "Now get out. I am going to get dressed."

My opening move in this game of deception was what I was going to wear to the banquet. Cormorant wanted me to wear a dress. He'd picked it out for me. He still thought me perfect and weak and in need of protection. I didn't know whether playing into that expectation would fit my plan, because I didn't yet have a plan, and in the absence of a conflicting conviction, I decided to simply go along with what the governor wanted for now. Right. I had to get them used to my rhythm, then surprise them with the right hook. This dress would be my jab. Every smile and nod would be a jab. The hook could come later.

An apple-cheeked servant who was always smiling helped me dress. She babbled about how happy she was that I had returned (for the governor's sake) as she strapped me into this garment that fit like it was made for the woman I was two months ago, not the one I was now. It was too tight everywhere that I had put on muscle or fat, which was pretty much my whole body, pinching me with sharp wrinkles on my shoulders. The corset pushed into my ribcage, and I did not like how constraining or heavy it was. It would be hard to run in. The servant brushed and oiled my hair, painted over all of my cuts and bruises with makeup, and told me all the while how beautiful I still looked, as though I were in need of reassurance after everything that had happened to me. I bore her pity with tight lips, waiting for it to be over.

When the servant propped me up in front of the mirror, I almost didn't recognize myself. My baby fat was gone, making me look a good deal more mature. I was more sharp in the face than I'd ever been before, and I turned left and right in the mirror to admire the angles of my cheeks. I loved the look of my shoulders pushing against the tight sleeves of my dress like they were too strong to be constrained, even though I knew I wasn't nearly as strong as Ama or Zayne or someone who had been sailing for a lot longer. The dress looked like it was made for someone else, but I liked that. It shouldn't fit me anymore.

When I left my room, I discovered that my door was guarded by a pair of navy men in their starchy uniforms, who looked at me with distrust and followed me as I made my way towards the main hall. I was still trying to think as I walked. My working plan was to tell the governor that Toussaint had saved my life, perhaps adapting the story of when he had jumped off the *Triton* into the ocean to save me. Perhaps that would be enough to earn him a little mercy, but then I entered the hall.

The hall was most of the way through a transformation—preparing for some kind of celebration. Everything was decorated in white. Drooping lace garlands hung from the rafters, and flower petals dappled the floor. The tables had all been removed and replaced with benches. Many more guests than I expected were standing around: local dignitaries who I didn't know. The room looked like it was set up for a wedding. I looked down at the lacy white dress that I was wearing with a sharpening sense of horror.

"No, you're not supposed to be here yet!" The governor ran up to me, beaming. He wore a new suit. His eyes were red and wet from crying.

"What is this?" I asked, dreading the answer that I already knew.

The governor took my hands in his. "Do you remember, right before you were taken, I told you I had half a mind to marry you that night? Well, in the weeks since, I have cursed myself for not marrying you the second I laid my eyes on you. I should have, I knew it, and because of our waiting—" He choked off, with the sound of a sob, even though his toothy smile barely faltered. "If I had, if you were sleeping in my bed that night, then I could have kept you safe. I swore I would never let another thing happen to you. So, as an apology for keeping you waiting, we are not going to wait a single day more!"

My smile sharpened into one of glass. It reflected the governor's joy back at him, while everything underneath became cold and clear.

"I wouldn't have it any other way," I told him.

I kept up my glass smile throughout the whole wedding ceremony. I didn't need to tell some grand lie to ingratiate myself; I only needed to reflect Cormorant's expectations back at him. I smiled as I walked down the aisle at sunset. I met him before the minister. I took his hands. I said 'I do,' and I kissed him. He slid his tongue between my lips with an invasive force built up over weeks and weeks of obsession. I winced at the slug in my mouth while the room cheered behind me, but the glass smile was back to greet my husband once it was over.

At the banquet, I nibbled at the foods, pretended that I liked them, and smiled blankly at the guest dignitaries and friends of the governor. I overheard one of them refer to me as 'a lovely girl; simple, but lovely,' and that's exactly how I wanted it. I smiled and nodded and slipped carving knives up the sleeves of my wedding dress.

He took me to his bedroom, always having two hands on me: on my neck and my hand, or both on my lower back, or on my shoulders, or in my hair. Outside of his bedroom, he took my head in his hands and kissed me again, even longer and deeper in my mouth. I heard his breath catch with arousal, and he moved on to kiss my neck and under my ear.

"Sir," I put my hands on his chest, trying to push him back.

"Don't call me sir," he said with heavy breath. "I'm your husband now; you should call me John."

"John," I said, feeling awkward about how that name felt. "We aren't in private."

"The hallway is empty."

"I know, but, decorum."

The governor chuckled at my demure act. "Of course, whatever my love wants, I will provide." And he opened the door to his bedroom.

The bed was sprinkled with flower petals. I walked around it, towards the governor's desk, as he closed the heavy door behind us. He crawled atop the bed to get to me, but before he could, I spoke to him.

"Sir—John—could I make a request of you?"

"Of course, darling, anything in the world will be yours."

"I want you to write a bill of pardon for Bad Weather."

Cormorant's expression changed from love to hate so quickly that it put me in the mind of Tlaloc, swapping out masks and moods as sudden as a change in the weather.

"That scum—" my husband began.

"He saved my life," I interrupted. "One night in a storm—"

"I do not care; whatever danger he put you in—"

"He risked his own life—"

"My sweetheart," he pet at my chin, "You are too good for this world, to want well even for a villain such as he. But don't you see I could never in my life sleep well again if I knew he was free to come and take you from me? You must understand—"

"I could not sleep again if I knew he had died because of me—"

"He has not died because of you," he snarled with hate again. "It has got nothing to do with anything you have done or could have done. You are an angel, and he is a devil—it is as simple as that. And he WILL be exorcised. You may be capable of forgiveness the likes of which I cannot fathom, but I am not." He breathed in deep, replacing his rage with arousal in a moment. "Now, enough of this talking. We shouldn't, either of us, be sleeping tonight."

I put a halting hand on his chest the next time that he bent over at me. He seemed surprised that I was strong enough to hold him up.

"If you don't write the pardon, I will leave and sleep in my own room tonight."

"You will do no such thing. You and I are never sleeping apart again for as long as I breathe."

I pushed him back onto the bed, then walked around towards the door. He hopped up in front of me and put a hand atop the doorknob to hold it shut.

"Mariah, dear, be reasonable."

"You said that you would do anything for me."

"Not that."

"Then let me out."

"You aren't leaving on our wedding night. You aren't leaving my side ever again."

I sighed and stepped back from the door. I wasn't gifted with lies and manipulation, but I'd thought that I would try anyway. Now, it was time for the other plan. I walked around to the far side of the governor's bed, again beside his desk. He relaxed a little as I left the door, but kept guard in front of it.

"Come here," I commanded him.

"Yes dear," the governor said with a smile, and again crawled across the bed to get to me.

I seized him by the necktie and kissed him on the mouth. He received the advance with obvious pleasure, but as he reached around my head to pull me in deeper, I pushed him backwards, so that he landed on his back on his bed. He grinned as I crawled up over him, straddling his waist and holding him down with a hand on his chest.

"I never thought…" he said, "But I like it."

Then I pressed a knife to his throat. I set the flat of the blade against his flesh, tight and cold, and pushed his neck up and backwards.

"Dear, that's a bit much," he said, and as he tried to push back, I cut him. It was a warning sting, not a murder cut, and it stilled him.

"Move and I will kill you," I warned. I pitched my voice low and cold, to make it clear to him that I was serious. "Shout out and I will kill you."

He laughed nervously. "You couldn't kill a fly."

"I have killed three men," I said coolly. "If you don't want to make it four, you will need to write me that bill of pardon for Toussaint Dupuis."

"*Him*," the governor snarled. "This isn't you, dear. He stole you, tricked you, turned you into—"

"He didn't steal me, John. I ran away because I didn't want to marry you. I wanted to become a pirate, and now I am one." I pushed him back into the pillow with my knife as he tried to struggle his way out. "I will kill you if you make me." I warned him. "I will make a forgery of your hand and use your seal and leave you dead on this bed. Don't make me. Write the letter."

The governor blubbered, "You are my wife. We are married."

"What do you think that matters to a lawless woman? Get it annulled tomorrow. Now, the pardon."

When I let him up to go to his desk, the governor decided to test me. He ran at me desperately, with his arms up and wide, clearly having never had a fight in his life. He lunged for the hand with the knife, but I just intercepted with the blade, and cut his arm so deeply that it stopped working. While he was reeling back from that wound, I pressed the knife point up under his chin.

"Test me again," I warned him. I stepped back and flicked the bloody knife down towards the desk. "Now write."

The governor was a coward. Underneath all of his promises of protection was a deep, omnipresent fear. I had seen before how he'd allowed himself to become consumed by the fear of losing that which he held precious; no doubt, his own life would have a place on his list of precious things. His fear made him sit down, with my knife on the back of his neck, and write out a full pardon for the pirate Bad Weather, and an order for his immediate and unconditional release. When the governor splattered some of his blood on the paper, I made him start writing again from the beginning. He sealed the letter with the wax crest of his office.

I collected sheets from the bed, ropes from the curtains, and belts from the closet, and used them all to bind the governor to the chair. I tied a small bandage around his arm, just enough to keep him from dying of blood loss. I shoved socks into his mouth and tied the gag behind his face with a scarf. My wedding dress was stained on the sleeves with blood, so I discarded it. I spun Cormorant in his chair to face the wall while I raided his closet for something new to wear.

The clothes that I stole this time were a good deal nicer than the last time: navy trousers, and a striped vest and jacket. I scrubbed the makeup off of my face, and hid my hair under a nice hat, and then I looked like a rich young gentleman. Lastly, I stole the governor's purse, which he had left on his bedside for the wedding, and hopped out the window into the night.

I ran to the prison. A drunken pair of young men were being booked as I arrived, yelling obscenities at each other and each saying that the other one should be punished for their collective crimes. I pushed by them to speak to the constable in charge.

"This is from the governor," I said, pitching my voice low as I slid the letter onto the table. "He has just been married and was moved to mercy from it."

The constable looked at the letter for a long time, his gigantic mustache wobbling with a frown. The wait made me nervous, so I took a silver coin from my new purse and slid it onto his desk. I added, in a hushed voice, "The governor would like this handled quickly and quietly and without questions."

The warden took the coin, shrugged, and pocketed it.

"Take him."

The cell in which I found Toussaint was disgusting: little more than a slime-filled pit, buzzing with flies. It smelled worse than a latrine. I did not like to think about what the slime used to be. I saw Toussaint by the window, with his face in the bars, looking forlornly out into the moonlight.

I opened up the cage and told him, "You're free to go."

When he saw me, Toussaint looked distraught. "I don't deserve it," he said without leaving his window. "I've once again dragged you—"

"Toussaint, just get out of there," I said. I had used up all of my patience on the governor, and didn't want to listen to him dither about his guilty conscience. "It stinks."

Toussaint gave me such a frank look of affection that I had to blush and look away. As he came out from the cell, he put a gentle hand on my shoulder, said thank you, and walked out with me. Together, we made our way back towards the docks, to where the *Argonaute* waited to leave at first light.

Eleven for the Devil, His Own Self

The *Argonaute* pulled into the harbor at Grande-Terre—the largest of the Guadeloupe islands—at dusk after many days at sea. We could just barely spy our final destination, Marie-Galante, from the deck of our ship as a shadowy lump on the sea. Toussaint frowned at the squat shape of it, with his knuckles tensing against the back railing, but this was as close as we were going to get to his father tonight; we would have to wait until the next day to find someone to ferry us across the water to the smaller island. I took Toussaint by the hand and pulled him away with me, down to town for a stroll, to loosen our legs and lessen his agitation.

The small settlement where we made landfall was called Pointe-à-Pitre, and I got the impression from the people who lived there that they couldn't make up their minds as to whether or not the settlement should keep existing. The town was full of abandoned or half-made buildings, all sunk down to various depths in the swampy ground. Often one corner of a structure would be deeper mired than the rest of it, so that the whole thing would tilt down in that direction, making wooden beams bend and crack from the strain of unplanned asymmetry. There were no obvious roads of stone or brick, only beaten-down paths through the mud, and quickly our boots became filled with gray goop. The men that we passed were all lonely laborers who were unhappy living in this back corner of the world, and they passed bottles of rum and wine back and forth to numb themselves to their loneliness. I didn't like how the mood of the place matched with Toussaint's brooding, but I had heard that alcohol was something that was used as a salve for nerves, so I dropped a little coin off at a tired-eyed trader's stand for a bottle of the terrible wine that seemed so popular with the locals.

Toussaint brightened up when I showed him the watery bottle. "You know that the path to my heart, my mouse, is paved with gifts both red and white."

"I'm afraid this is more of a brown than a red."

"'Tis appreciated nonetheless." He sipped from the bottle and gave a grimace. "Aye, but it is a drink fit for a pouring out on my grave."

"Don't speak like that," I said, slapping his arm a little. "You have many days ahead of you, and many drinks much better than that one."

"I am not so sure." Toussaint looked away from me. "I have that sense, again, that tomorrow is going to be an unlucky day for me. I think that it might very well be my last one on this earth. There is a storm coming on, and, madman that I am, I am again charging straight at it."

"You know that I'm not going to stand aside and let you die tomorrow, right?"

Toussaint chuckled to himself. "Ah, of course not. You are the only one I've ever known to be so mad as I, to know a storm is ahead and to charge headlong into it. I know how the rush of storm-winds fills your ears and chills your skin and numbs you to dangers and pains even as they conspire to destroy you. It's a terrifying power, that madness, but it doesn't make us immortal."

"You don't know that we aren't immortal," I said, trying to speak lightly. "I haven't died yet, and neither have you."

"Ah, if only," he said with a sad smile. We walked for a little bit, passing the bottle back and forth. "If I do die tomorrow."

"Toussaint..."

"*If* I do, I want to ask something of you: I want you to return to Tortuga. The *Villainelle* is bound to return there eventually. You know where my treasure is hidden; I want you to take the jewels and make a life for yourself, whatever life you want, wherever you want it to be."

"If you're dying, then I'll be dying with you."

"I know that is your stance on things," Toussaint said somberly. "I should not have brought you all the way out here. I'm sorry for it. It was a selfish thing. It is just that I like your company, and I don't know that I'd have the strength to make the journey without you."

"It's okay. I like your company too." I took his hand in mine, taking a breath for patience. He needed to say it; that's who he was. "I chose it. I want to be with you."

"Just as I want to be with you."

Toussaint looked like he was close to saying something more, but hid the message in another swig from the bottle, never to be seen again. He grimaced, blinked, and then it was gone.

It was a small town, and we soon circled the whole of it and returned to the ship from whence we had departed.

"Let us off to bed," I said, taking the bottle out of Toussaint's hands. "If the old god has a storm planned for tomorrow, then I think we'd best be awake for it."

Toussaint followed me up the gangplank. We shared a room together in the hold, but he waited in the mess area outside of our room. His journal was waiting for him on the table, and he took it up in his hands.

"You go ahead to bed," he told me. "I have some thoughts to get out of my head before I can sleep."

I frowned. "Don't stay up too late."

"Never, dear," he said with a smile.

I lay awake in bed that night for a long while. Over the past fortnight, I had gotten used to falling asleep beside him, forehead to forehead, and when I'd wake up, I would find my limbs entwined with his, without the slightest idea which of us had drawn the other in while we slept. This night, falling asleep without him, I slept fretfully and dreamed of loss.

In the morning, he wasn't there. No intertwined limbs. No cloud of raven hair. No smell of him on the pillow. All that was in its place was a sheet of paper ripped from his notebook.

Groggy-eyed and confused, I raised the paper up.

It was a portrait...of me, I realized after a moment. I hardly recognized myself. Toussaint had drawn me like I was some kind of heroine: with a sword on my hip, hair fluttering in the wind, square shoulders and confident jut of the chin. What I really recognized was my expression: a certain twist of my mouth, which I would give to Toussaint when he was being difficult. It was a look of affectionate disapproval. The girl in the portrait was so strong in her profile, but the look...it was pure, precious affection.

On the back, he'd written a poem—a villanelle—and titled it "to she whom I love."

My love, you are a force of nature, as strong
In your heart as the god whose curse I bear,
But I am too weak to bring you along.

I only made it through one stanza before erupting from the bed in a rage.

I ran out of my room with the paper crushed in one hand. He wasn't there. I ran up top. He wasn't there either. I cursed his name, cursed his mother, cursed everything that I could think to curse as I ran down the deck, down the gangplank, looking everywhere for a sign of him. Even after everything I'd said, after every time that I'd assured him it was my choice to be in danger with him, he had taken that choice away from me. He'd left me behind while he went to confront his father and the damned god alone.

I ran down the quay in search of missing boats, only to find a group of men bickering about a theft in the night: one of their boats had been stolen. I butted in and asked them if they knew when the theft occurred, if it was late last night or early this morning, but they couldn't tell me, so I cursed again and spun back around.

The sky was already gray and the climate cold and windy as I hunted around for someone who could take me across to Marie-Galante. The dock was full of ships, but most of their sailors looked up at the ominous sky and told me, no, I'd better wait for clearer weather. Storms around these parts can come on sudden, they said, and although Marie-Galante tends to be spared the worst, if I'm out in the middle of the water when a big one hits, I won't make it to the other side. I cursed, apologized, and kept looking.

Finally, I found a handsome young man who said he was happy to make some coin on a day when he wasn't going to get any fishing done.

The man had blonde hair down to his shoulders, and gave me many smiles, and I think wanted more than just some coin from me, but I was desperate, so I agreed to ride with him, keeping my hand on the hilt of the carving knife in my belt as we crossed the water.

The sky darkened as we went, and we heard the distant call of thunder many times. I had a terrible feeling that I was too late already, and a big part of me wanted to seize control of the oars of this little dinghy and force us to go faster. Instead, I took out Toussaint's crumpled poem and read over the rest of it.

It was a love poem. A love poem? From him? To me? I didn't understand. I read it again, as the rain began to fall and mark the paper in scattered drops. It was a goodbye as well. He was expecting to die today, and he loved me, so he wouldn't let me follow him. I cursed again and wiped my wet arm across my eyes. He loved me? How did he mean? Did he mean, romantically? Or as a friend? These are the foolish thoughts that I wondered and then discarded, instead simply resolving that I needed to find him and save him from his own foolishness.

We landed near the town of St. Louis, but it was raining when we arrived, and the dirt roads were empty of people. I slipped away from my boat guide when he tried to coax me into a tryst at the town tavern. I ran down the empty streets, looking for someone, anyone.

A couple of women were standing in the shade of a roof, wrapped in shawls, and looking northwards with concern. I approached them with the intent of asking questions, but their conversation was heated.

They spoke in French: "[Why couldn't it have waited until tomorrow, is what I want to know. Up at the top there, the wind alone is a menace. And the rain, Bert'll be sniffling about a cold all night long, you mark my words.]"

"[They'll be done soon enough. I'm sure Dupuis will be quick about it.]"

Their rapid conversation difficult for me to parse, as their French was a far cry from the Parisian dialect that I had studied, but I clearly recognized the name "Dupuis," and came rushing up once I heard it.

"Excuse-moi," I spoke to them in French. "[Could you tell me has something gone on?]"

The women looked at each other. "[The crier just came through, did you sleep through him? Can't imagine that.]"

"[I did,]" I said, to speed the conversation along. "[What did he say?]"

"[Why, only that there was an attempt on the governor's life in the night. The criminal was caught and taken up to the Maw. The whole militia's had to go up and watch, which I was just telling her was nonsense...]"

I was already gone, on my way up the hill in the direction they pointed.

Great limestone cliffs wrapped around the northern coast of the island, rising 50-100 feet above sea level in some spots, and making the coast there unapproachable from the water. It was a long but steady journey to reach these cliffs, on a road made of the same chalky limestone as the cliffs themselves. The road was well-stomped down by many feet, for the journey was one that men of the village had to make often. Ever since Dupuis became governor of Marie-Galante, all criminals had been marched up this road, with the assembled militia about them, to reach the sight of their execution: "Gueule Grande Gouffre" or "The Great Maw."

The wind grew stronger and stronger the higher I ran up the road, making the occasional heavy raindrops feel like missiles from a great god's bow. Towards the top, the view to the storm front became clearer, and I could see the clouds as an encroaching titan, slowly twisting around itself as it lumbered ever closer. It would soon become very dangerous to be standing in the open air atop these cliffs.

The Maw was a great, cylindrical chasm, a hundred feet deep, with smooth white walls going down to a circular saltwater lagoon. Long before France settled this island, the limestone bedrock under the cliffs had collapsed in on itself here just inside of the cliff line, creating a gigantic sinkhole. The wall between the round lagoon and the sea eroded further over the centuries or millennia until part of the wall collapsed into the chasm. Now, what was once a cliff wall had become a rocky archway over a window to the sea. A pair of great limestone pillars made of the fallen chunks of cliff jutted out into the middle of this window, looking like a pair of fangs in the mouth of a snake.

The road ended on the south side of the Maw's rim, near a man-made stage that rattled in the wind. This stage was trussed out over the maw, so that it rested half on stone and half on empty air. It was wide and flat, without railings or stairs or walls: a launching point from which criminals could be dropped.

The assembled militia stood around the stage, less than a dozen of them, all unarmed and dressed in whatever ordinary clothes they would wear as a fisher or a carpenter or a farmer, for they only worked as militiamen when called to, and nine days in ten they were only civilians. Many of them appeared to be regretting their part-time occupation today, as they stared out glumly at the approaching storm and muttered prayers to slow it down. None noticed or cared to stop me as I pushed past them to get a better view of the stage.

A man was making a speech, reading with a voice that was lost in the wind from a paper that flapped heavily in his hands. He was dressed finely, like a noble, with an ornamental rapier tied to his hip. He faced the storm with his back to the crowd, making entreaties up to the sky. An executioner stood by with his black hood over his face and a woodcutter's axe over his shoulder. The prisoner was bound atop a plank over the Maw, and the sight of him filled me with despair.

Toussaint's mouth was gagged and bound with ropes around his hands, and his arms, and his feet. The ropes around his feet bound him to a chipped millstone, which looked heavy enough that most men wouldn't be able to lift it alone. A taut rope connected the far end of the plank on which Toussaint stood to an iron cleat on the stand. The rope was what was keeping the plank pointed straight out, and when it was severed, it would drop the plank down, and Toussaint with it, all the way down fifty or a hundred feet into the lagoon below.

The speech finished with a flourish, and the nobleman stepped back to make way for the hooded executioner and his axe. I broke away from the crowd of militia, who were not so alert as to even really look at me as I pushed past them, until I was all the way on the stage.

"Arrêt!" I screamed at the executioner, my shrill voice cutting through the wind. In French, I shouted, "[Stop this! Don't you know who that is? That's the governor's son.]"

The executioner halted, and the well-dressed man turned to me with surprise and rage frank on his face.

"[I am the governor,]" he said. "[Who are you?]"

The governor wore a hood to protect him from the rain, but, underneath it, he looked very little like his son. His eyes were sunken in dark shadows, and he wore a pair of thick glasses over them that magnified his eyes. He looked boney in his cheeks, and when he blinked, muscles all down his cheeks twitched at once, so that it felt like he was blinking with his whole face.

"Dupuis?" I asked. "[Do you know that's your own son?]" I pointed at Toussaint.

"[It is a lie,]" the governor answered, blinking his eyes and twitching his nose. "[I ask again—]"

"[It is the truth, I swear it]," I said. The executioner stepped backwards from the rope, his hood turned in towards Dupuis with a querying tilt as I spoke. "[Do you not believe me, or are you a liar?]"

"[I have no son at all,]" Dupuis answered quickly. "[I had a daughter ten years ago, but she is dead now.]"

"[He left you ten years ago under a different name, but he is your blood.]" I walked closer, and as I did, the militia fell in closer around the stage.

"[Who the hell are you?]" he spat. "[I do not know you. You cannot know me and my family. Are you another pirate, hmm, like him? Are you his ally?]"

"[I am his friend, and I know his history, and yours, very well,]" I said, with a warning in my voice. "[I know that you sold your own son to the devil, and here you are trying to deliver.]"

The surrounding men gasped in various levels of disbelief, muttering to each other about whether they heard what I said correctly.

"[She is a pirate!]" Governor Dupuis shouted to the group, and, within his rage, I saw the furtive flailing of a man caught in a lie. "[She is a liar. She will say what she needs to save her kin.]"

"[My kin? He's your kin!]" I turned my attention to the gathered militia. "[People, please, this man is not who you think. The governor is a heathen, and a murderer. He makes blood sacrifices to a heathen god.]"

Dupuis hissed, "[Silence, wench.]"

"[Why do you think he has been having the executions up here, at this terrible Gueule? Don't you know that the old heathens would offer their sacrifices to their gods just like this? He drowns people to send them to Tlalocan as sacrifices to an evil god of the seas.]"

I called him a heathen in order to persuade the Christian men assembled there; however, I was a stranger, and a woman besides, so I was not entirely credible as a source. Belief and disbelief both flittered amongst the militiamen, but Dupuis knew the truth, and it panicked him to hear these accurate accusations thrust upon him.

"[Arrest her, Captain!]" Governor Dupuis commanded. "[She slanders my name. Jenson, take her!]"

The captain, Jenson, was the only member of the militia who had come up to the Maw with a weapon, and he seemed to treat his position with much more solemnity than did most of his fellows. He approached me on the stage without drawing his sword, not expecting much resistance from me.

"[I demand a trial!]" I exclaimed. "[I demand a stay of execution.]" I affixed my eyes on the slits in the executioner's hood. "[He does not deserve to die. Stay your hand or stain it with blood the likes of which cannot be washed off.]"

"[Kill him,]" Dupuis ordered the executioner. When his words did not produce immediate action, he squared off against the hooded man, staring him down. "[Now!]"

"[No, please,]" I pleaded, as the captain grabbed me from behind.

Captain Jenson thought that I was just some blubbering woman, not the kind to put up any sort of fight. When he grabbed me, I answered with an elbow to his gut that caught him completely by surprise. He bent over and I kneed him in the groin, punched him in his cheek, and again in his temple. He went from the proud captain of the militia to groaning on the ground in the space of a moment.

While I fought, the governor confronted the executioner. "[Do your duty.]"

The executioner shook his head. "[Monsieur, I'm a woodcutter. I don't have—]"

"[—the nerve,]" the governor finished scornfully. "[Then I'll do it myself.]"

Dupuis drew his rapier from its sheathe. It was only a decorative blade, but it was more than sharp enough to cut a rope.

"[Don't you dare,]" I shouted, stalking towards him from the downed form of the militia captain. "[I will kill you! Drop it!]"

"[At last, I send you to hell,]" he yelled, and raised his sword, and thunder struck, and rain fell in like a bucket emptying onto our heads. The hurricane had finally reached us.

I ran forward as Dupuis swung down at the rope, and hit it, and severed it, and sent Toussaint, wide-eyed, down backwards into the maw. The pirate did a little hop, as if he could jump back to the safety of the stage with his feet tied together, but then the millstone caught on its tether and yanked him down with it into the chasm. I ran and dove for the rope in some vain hope of catching it, but it was far too late. I watched him fall, and despair wrung my heart.

Dupuis swung his sword at me, but I saw it coming out of the corner of my eye. I spun and scurried up to my feet, back in towards the center of the stage. The governor growled, wide-eyed with rage, and attacked me with his sword a second time. The governor swung without any artful training like that of the inquisitor on board *El Sabueso*; he only swung like an ordinary man with intent to murder.

Madness struck me. Everything slowed down. Blood pumped itself through my veins with a heavy sluggishness that brought heat to my extremities. I drew the carving knife from my belt and blocked Dupuis' attack in one motion. I had to get to Toussaint. Dupuis was in my way. He said something more to me, but I couldn't understand it. Maddening blood had entered my ears and deafened me to the rest of the world, to the waves and the winds, and the taunts of the governor.

I could not hear the order that he barked at his waiting militiamen, but I saw the opening in his guard.

I swung my knife through his neck, and his eyes widened. He fell to his knees and dropped his sword as the blood bubbled out from the cut.

"[Die slowly,]" I told him, and put away my knife, and looked out off the edge of the stage.

Madness redoubled its numbing influence. Thought would betray my resolve, so I ended my thoughts. I only held space in my mind for one simple action—to move forward. The blood in my ears deafened me to my own footfalls, as I ran straight out towards the chasm, fast enough that by the time I saw how steep the drop was, I could not stop myself from jumping.

I fell both faster and slower than I expected. In two seconds, I was in the water, but getting there was a long time. I remember thinking that I was dead. I floated like a ghost in mid-air as every snippet of information I'd ever heard about surviving a fall from a great height into water flashed through my mind. Storm-winds thrashed about me, the tumbling ocean beneath. The many frothing waves reached up to me like a crowd of begging fingers, clamoring up to seize me and drag me under. I struck my flailing legs together into one knife blade, aiming to punch a hole in the water for the rest of me to fall into.

As I fell, Tlaloc launched a bolt of lighting down into the spot where I had just been, which crashed into the stage above me, and ended in a moment my wish for Dupuis to die slowly. The sound was a crack and a crash, and it made me spin myself half-way around to get a look at it as my feet hit water.

A bit of the surface clipped my chin and sent my neck popping backwards as I plunged down deep underwater. The moment that I came to rest felt reminiscent of being suspended in Apan, on the way to Tlalocan, as I was unsure what way was up and what way was down. Then half of the lightning-struck stage fell into the water above me, in a great crater that rocked me with its force. I fought the instinct to immediately flail upwards for the surface. Instead, I swam downwards, looking around in search of Toussaint. My neck would only turn one way—turning to the right sent great pains up the side—but I saw him down at the bottom of another trail of bubbles, in a cloud of murk that he stirred up in his panic.

Toussaint was sawing desperately at the rope that bound his feet with the sharpest rock he could find, but he was not making progress. It was quite dark down there, a good 30 feet underwater, but I could see the ominous remains of previous criminals as shadows on the floor of the lagoon. Toussaint was close to joining them. He was already drowning, his chest spasming and his head flinching back and forth as he struggled to keep himself from breathing.

I grabbed Toussaint's shoulder, and he jumped in surprise, dropping his rock from his bound hands. He looked at me in shock, and some kind of complicated emotion that was torn between begging me to leave and thanking me for coming. I didn't give his expression the time it would take to dissect it. Instead, I crawled down his body, pulling myself hand over hand down to the ropes around his feet.

My lungs were already burning with lack of air before I even started cutting into the ropes, but I knew that I only had one chance to free him. I drew my knife and, in doing so, released a small, bloody cloud into the clear water. I pushed it into the ropes that tied him to the millstone and sawed back and forward. It only took a few seconds to sever each rope, but those seconds were precious; I kept cutting ropes as my vision sparkled with blackness, as my lungs bucked in my chest, and as Toussaint relinquished his last breath above me. He was terribly still as I sliced through the last rope, and, once freed, he only floated in place without swimming for the surface.

I kicked off from the limestone floor, pulling Toussaint upwards with me. I spasmed as I swam, every survival instinct begging me to surface as fast as I could. Even as I rose, my vision dimmed, and grew darker, as if I were sinking and not rising. My hands curled into claws as I pulled against the water with open fingers that could tear into flesh but only let water pass through them.

We broke the surface into the rain, and I gasped and coughed out the water that I had inhaled. Toussaint didn't. I struggled to keep his face above water as I spun around, searching for something to hold on to in the water which swirled around itself in a tumult like a great sloshing bowl in the hands of a giant. I spied a great slab of the stage, buoying up and down in the surf. I slung an arm into Toussaint's bindings and tugged him along the gray waves towards it. I flung him up onto the pallet, where he slapped down as motionless as a dead fish.

I cursed, with my feet dangling off the wood, as there was no room aboard for both of us to lie side by side. I tugged the gag down from his mouth, cursed again, and called into his ear.

"Toussaint," I said, and slapped his cheek. "Toussaint, Bad Weather, can you hear me?"

He had drowned in the maw of the god of the sea. His soul was lost to Tlalocan.

"It's not too late," I said tearfully. "It can't be too late."

He may be in Tlalocan, but I knew the way out of it. We had traveled there together, and left together. I pressed my lips to his and pushed air into his lungs. Saltwater answered, filling my mouth with is iron-tinged taste. I spat out the water, and breathed into him again, and again, shoving against his chest as I went to push more of the water out.

Toussaint came to life with a sudden surge of energy. He coughed and wheezed and coughed again.

My relief made me so light-headed that I could have fainted right there and slipped down into the water. "Thank god," I muttered.

As I pulled Tlaloc's sacrifice back out from his domain, I felt a great answering rumble in the earth. The rocks shook with his anger; cracks ran up the twin serpent fang pillars that marked the gate to the sea and sent great chunks of limestone falling into the water.

"I am sorry," is the first thing Toussaint said to me.

"Shut up," I told him, as I hurried to cut off his other bindings. "Are you okay? Can you move?"

"Yes, I do think so," he answered, flexing his newly freed fingers.

"Good," I said, and I smacked him on the head. "You goddamn fool. You think I'm just going to turn around and leave you, idiot? You think I'm going straight away to run to Tortuga, just because you told me to?"

"I am sorry," he coughed.

"Shut up!" I told him. "Did you ever think that maybe, just maybe, the reason that I keep coming after you, and why I won't let you shake me, might be that I love you too, idiot? Do you think you can just not give me a chance to say it back? So don't you dare play with my heart and say that it was some kind of poetic turn of phrase and you didn't mean it like I mean it, because I have done this, all of this, because I love you. You understand? So do you love me?"

"Of-of course," he stammered.

"And you love me like a man loves a woman, not just like a friend, not just—"

"Mariah, I love you in every way a man can love a woman."

It felt absurd how that could fill me with butterflies while I treaded water, hanging from the side of a soot-singed stage in the middle of a storm, but it did. My stomach dropped, heavy with affection and longing, when I was already so full of other emotions. Too many things were happening, and they made me feel like crying. I wiped my eyes.

"Then we are getting out of this damn hole," I said, and subjugated my feelings to that goal.

The walls of the Gueule Grande Gouffre were very smooth; climbing up them would be a challenging undertaking under the best of circumstances, and these circumstances were far from the best. The rain had slickened every bit of the limestone, and now the walls were so slippery that we couldn't find purchase enough to even begin to climb up. Our only hope was to swim out of the lagoon, between the twin snake fang pillars and out through the window to the sea. The cliffs just outside would still be too steep to climb, but if we could swim along the coast for a mile or so without being pulled out by the tide, we should be able to eventually find a place where climbing out was possible.

That was our plan as we swam across to the pillars, but what we didn't notice was that the whole time that we were arguing—ever since the great shaking of the earth—the water in which we swam had been sinking lower. It was draining out somewhere, and it wasn't until we were swimming by the snake-fang pillars that we noticed. By then, the water level had fallen so low that a rocky bar had appeared across the exit to the sea. As we pulled ourselves up onto it, we finally saw where all the water had gone.

It was a great wave as wide as the world.

The first time that Toussaint and I had done battle with a storm together, I had sensed an unexplainable malevolence in the wind. That was nothing compared to what I sensed from this wave. This wave was to be a punishment as complete and unavoidable as the eagles sent to pluck out Prometheus' liver. The distant roar of water was the same as the call of the angry giant who chased jack down the beanstalk, and we had no axe to stop it with. This was fate. We were going to die.

I reached down to hold Toussaint's hand, thinking only to spend my last minute with him.

"We need to get to higher ground," Toussaint said, breaking me from my hypnotic acceptance.

"How?" I asked.

Toussaint looked to the twin fangs. They were craggier than the walls of Gueule Grande, and tapered as they went upward so that the angle at which we would have to climb was not so sheer as that of the cliff wall. They were not so tall that we could climb completely out of the hole with them, but we wouldn't have time anyway to reach the top before the wave arrived. I gave Toussaint a nod, and together we began to climb the closer of the two pillars.

Toussaint was a much faster climber than I was. He had an incredible sense of balance and sureness of step, and no discernable fear of falling. He stopped every few steps to offer me a hand up, and make sure that I continued with him. I kept looking back behind me as I climbed, hugging the wall with both hands and trembling as I watched the wave grow ever closer.

We were a little more than half-way up when the wave hit. It exploded in a big geyser when it hit our pillar, sending up intense tremors and a deluge of water. I held on tight to the pillar as water rushed into the maw beneath us. After surviving the initial strike, up where we were, it seemed safe for a moment. Then the Maw opened.

I heard a great roar, and the rock under our feet shifted down all at once. The water in the Maw began to spin around in a big spiraling whirlpool. Big chunks of flotsam rolled around, mixing with dirt and silt, and making the water appear black and impenetrable. These murderous chunks of sharp things were drawn closer and closer to a hole in the middle of the spiral, then they disappeared deep underwater, never to resurface. It was the great, gulping mouth of the god made manifest, to swallow us up and drag us into Apan.

The other fang cracked at its base and fell forward into the Maw. As it hit, it sent up a great splash that crashed into us; then our fang began to shudder and crack under our fingers. I reached out and grabbed ahold of Toussaint's hand as our fang suffered a great jolt and then tilted in towards the Maw. I jammed my other hand into a crack in the rock, holding on like my life depended on it as our fang fell beneath the water's surface.

The current of the whirlpool was very strong and swift and it pulled most of my body off of the rock with it, but I kept holding on to the crack. Our fang settled so that the back half of it remained out of the water, and my crack was just barely under the surface, so while the water kept trying to push me down and drown me, I could still just barely breathe.

Toussaint wasn't so lucky. He fell off as he hit the water, and only barely managed to keep a hold of my hand. The current tried to pull him away from me, just as it tried to pull me from my hand, but I held on. He grabbed my wrist with his second hand, and I tried to pull him in. It felt like I was playing a game of tug of war against the god of the sea, and Toussaint was my rope. As all the water drained out from this reality and emptied into the infinite seas of Apan, I heard the call from Tlalocan, in the voice of the red mask: "**MINE!**"

"You can't have him!" I yelled out into the storm. "He's mine. Mine! And you can't take him from me."

Toussaint's grip weakened. I looked into his face, and he looked back at mine, and I saw a very familiar expression.

"Don't you dare," I yelled at him. "You are mine. You are not allowed. You let go, and I follow you, and I die. Is that what you want? No? Then live, dammit!"

I don't think that he heard everything that I said, because I certainly didn't hear what he said back, but I think he understood the threat. He grabbed me again with both hands, and let me keep pulling him closer. I don't know where I got the strength from. I must have the blood of a goddess somewhere far back in my lineage, because I felt a surge of strength come from a wellspring deep within me. It felt like this strength had been waiting my whole life for a test against the divine. I drank deeply from that well and used its strength to pull Toussaint close enough to the pillar that he could find his own crack to grab onto.

The water level lowered as it drained out into the endless Apan. Eventually, it became low enough that we could pull ourselves up onto the rock again. Once the whirlpool current slowed a little, and we were solidly on rock for long enough that immediate death seemed unlikely, Toussaint seized me about the shoulders and pulled me into him.

"You have me," he cried into my shoulder. "I'm yours."

I held him back. "You're mine," I said, feeling a desperate need to bring him into me and to hold him as closely as I could. I wanted to pull him so close that we would meld into one body, and so keep him safe with me.

We huddled together while we waited for the storm to end, making good use of the magic whereby two people, each themselves cold, can nonetheless warm each other just by being together. It took what felt like hours for the pull of the whirlpool to dissipate. We were safe atop our boulder for the rest of it; the defeated god had enough honor not to try another trick, now that I had beaten them in a test of strength. Once it was over, the water in the lagoon was much shallower than it had been before, as chunks of rock filled up the hole and closed the door to Apan.

Tlaloc's great mouth was stuck up with rocks, his portal collapsed, and his high priest deceased.

I felt so weak after using all of my strength that I dozed on Toussaint's shoulder until he nudged me awake, when the rain was down to a drizzle. He directed me to look out through the stony arch, to where a rainbow touched down on the ocean. I thought it was so strange. We had seen so many storms during my time in the Caribbean, yet this was the first time I could remember seeing a rainbow. It felt like a good omen at last.

An end to Bad Weather.

Epilogue

This was the end of our bad luck. Toussaint and I continued to sail together. At first, we returned to the Villainelle, but then we struck out on our own. We made enough of a fortune to settle in a North American city (not going to say which one), and founded our own printing press. We married, and live together as a family with our son, whose adoption is its own story. I write and print, while Toussaint has gotten himself involved with politics. He is an advocate for abolition and independence, and I edit and publish his pamphlet for him.

I don't know that I will ever release this story. Maybe after my death. For now, it's only something that demanded that I write it down. Now, after it has been so much time since these events occurred, I find myself wondering how much of it really happened. I have my journals from that time—my own accounts of gods and monsters—but I have no memory of Tlaloc's face. I only remember the feelings. The feelings were genuine.

Our luck is ordinary now. Our lives are ordinary. It feels like I'm lying to my neighbors when I chat with them over little things and don't tell them of the wonders I've witnessed or the people I've killed. I suppose that is also why I need to write my book. So that the truth will surface one day.

I am Mariah Goldenleaf. I love Toussaint Dupuis. I was a pirate. I may still technically be married to the governor of Jamaica (I haven't stopped by to check whether he ever did get that one annulled). I have killed. I have stolen. I have bested a god in a battle of strength. And I am free.

Acknowledgements

I first want to offer the biggest possible thanks to my family, whose support has been unwavering, and whose faith in me has been steadier than my faith in myself. Next I want to thank Faye Goodwin, who gave me feedback after every chapter, and helped me to make this book what it is now. Thank you so much to Monroe for the incredible cover art. Thanks to Madeline Farlow for the advice on taking this to publishing. Thanks to all of my other friends who have read and given feedback. Emily Smith. Danny Reiland. Quinn Baker. Cameron Hollister. Thanks to all my wonderful teachers at American University, especially Dolen, Stephanie, and David. Thanks to the Pirate History Podcast for being an entertaining source of historical context.

Coming soon...

If you enjoyed
AGAINST A SEA OF TROUBLES,
Read on for an excerpt from
<u>APOTERASIS:</u>
<u>DESCENT INTO THE MOUTH OF MONSTERS</u>
By JJD Thomas
Coming in Fall 2024
***

Find us at www.jjdthomas.com
***

As a note: *Apoterasis* is somewhat scarier than *Against a Sea of Troubles*. Whereas *AaSoT* is about 40% adventure, 30% romance, 20% history, 10% fantasy, *Apoterasis* is more like 60% fantasy, 30% horror, and 10% romance. Trigger warning for self-harm.

Apoterasis

Descent into the Mouth of Monsters

Apotheosis: (*noun*) the ascension of a mortal to godhood; to become divine

Apoterasis: (*noun*) the falling of a mortal to monstrosity; to become abominable

***

Chapter 1:
The Town at the Edge of the Abyss

***

I t wasn't as terrible as you'd think, growing up next to the Monsters' Mouth. It was rather beautiful, really. We called our town 'Sunflower Ridge,' because of how the hills were covered in happy yellow flowers. Every morning, I woke up to see a sea of blonde faces all bobbing at me gently from across the valley. The hills were so full of sweetgrass that the air smelled like candy, and our beautiful goats with their long white hair ate so much that they only ever laid around lazily. It was a lovely place to live, so long as you stayed up on the ridge.

I had a best friend, Colin, who was as blonde as the sunflowers. He had freckles all over his cheeks and a laugh like a bell chime. We played ball in the upper regions of the Mouth, kicking a sheep's bladder full of wool back and forth across the valley. I liked his laugh, and he liked my black-blue hair, and I was pretty sure that we would get married one day. He loved being outside, so even though I had terrible allergies, I let him drag me down the hills to play. The later we played, the more the ball would roll and bring us down with it, like a tide, deeper into the valley.

The Mouth had a funny kind of twist to it, where as soon as you reached wherever you thought was the lowest point in the valley, you'd look around and find another bend in the path, and another lower point further on ahead. We were told early, and repeatedly, not to go looking for the bottom, because we'd never find it.

Sometimes, our game took us all the way down to the shurtle village. Their domed huts of straw and mud blended in with the sides of the valley as they rose up at steeper angles. The shurtles were a peaceful kind of monster, looking like some kind of sheep-people with bushy white fur all around their faces. They never said a word, but only used a wordless gesture-speech to communicate. They waved at us when we came by, but gestured severely not to continue further down into the Mouth. It was dangerous, they signed.

We were eight years old when Colin caught the scent of something on the wind that smelled like roasted nuts. We followed the smell down past the shurtles to where the valley started to become so deep that it made no sense to call it a valley anymore, and it became more of a canyon. There, we found a big disk of stone, like a plate for a giant, covered with wonderful foods. It had loaves of toasted nut-bread and a whole smoked goat just sitting there. Shurtle nut-bread was a wonderful treat for us, so we took a roll each and ate crunchy bites while we kicked our ball back and forth across the slope.

The Mouth's floor was steeper here, and when the ball got away from us, it rolled, rolled, rolled far out of sight. Colin was the one who had kicked it, so he ran down to fetch it while I sat on the edge of the stone plate and drizzled honey from a pot onto another nut roll. The light yellowed around me as the sun dipped down over the canyon wall. Colin didn't come back. Once the yellow turned orange, I jumped off the plate and ventured down the valley, calling his name.

Down the path, I saw the silhouette of a giant. It sat on its heels, but was twice as tall in that posture as a man would be at his full height. Its knees bowed out to either side of a bulbous torso. Its arms had two elbows apiece, and eight webbed fingers at the end. Its back was turned to me at first, covered in long, slimy black hair. It turned its long snout to the side and lifted a limp, humanoid silhouette up to that snout, sunk its teeth in, and tore out a bite.

I froze. I couldn't breathe. I dropped my nut-roll. The froate blinked one big yellow-and-green eye at me, with a black pupil that was blocky like a goat's. I took one of my hands and dug my fingernails into the other elbow as deep as I could. I pierced through to blood, and the sudden sensation of pain brought me back to the present. I turned and I ran. I fell. I scrambled back up. I kept running…all the way back to the sunflower fields.

Colin was never seen again.

That was when I was eight years old. A lot of us up on the ridge had stories like that. We lived in a dangerous place, and not respecting its dangers came with consequences. It was a lesson that I took to heart, and without Colin to drag me outside, I spent most of the next few years indoors.

I spent most of my time weaving lace. I spun thin, silvery goat hair into cashmere threads, which I wove through pins stuck into my pillows. My first patterns were simple and geometric, but I soon taught myself how to weave pictures of flowers and animals and all sorts of beautiful things. When Ma showed me how to make the basic stitches, she'd intended for weaving to be a distraction from my grief, but she had no idea how much I would take to it. More than just a distraction, it gave me a sense of order and control. No matter what tragedies came to me, I could disappear into my lacework and the world would calm down while I put it all in order.

I became so wrapped up in my weaving that I shirked my household responsibilities, making my parents lose patience with me as the years went on. That changed when I was thirteen years old, and the ursavuul came to visit. I was sitting at the window, working on a sunflower pattern, when my mother called out to me from the kitchen.

"Miss Daisy Hemmings! Don't make me holler at you again!"

I looked up with a start from my work. I hadn't heard her hollering the first time. I hollered back, "What is it, Mama?"

"I said get on down here—are you dull?"

"I didn't hear you, Ma. I'm working."

"Working? Bah! That's not work. I'll give you some real work to do, get you learning what work is. Did I raise you kids not to know what work is? I ain't that sort of mother. Get on down here if you don't want me to come up there with a wallop."

I rolled my eyes at the window. Ma didn't respect my work very much. She called it a hobby and always said there were a thousand more important things I should be doing. I started to get upset with her for yelling at me, but I stabbed a pin into my palm instead of arguing back. The pain brought clarity and calm. It always did.

"Yes, Ma," I called back. I licked off the bead of blood that the pin made in my palm, then folded up a sheet over my work. I left it atop the box where I kept all of my laces. I smoothed out my skirt, which I'd dyed periwinkle with berries and embroidered with a lace scene of a little girl on a hill. It had taken me months to finish and was probably my favorite.

When I reached the kitchen, Ma was busy with her nonsense. I stood by, demurely, with my hands folded before me, and my head slightly bowed. "How can I help, Ma?"

She had me fetch a broom and use it to brush up all the little bits on the floor. I didn't see any little bits, but I bit my cheek and nodded and did what I was told. The kitchen was already clean, in my opinion—she was just making herself busy to keep from worrying. My father had left for town a while ago, to see about rumors of a monster come up from the Mouth. It had come during the daytime, which was unusual for a monster, and had seemed peaceful, but now it was nearly dusk and Pa still wasn't home yet. Ma went to yell at my brothers to get inside, but they were already on the mat when she opened the door. Everyone knew to be in before dark.

It was another hour still before Pa came home. Ma was watching from the window, and she yelped out when she saw him. She threw open the door, and my dad was standing there with a fist raised, ready to knock.

"Where have you..." Ma gasped. "What is that?"

Pa had a giant shadow standing behind him, whose black hair blended into the night. The beast ducked his head, so that he could see under the doorframe, and took off his wide-brimmed hat of red straw.

"Good evening, Ma'am," the ursavuul said in a low, low voice. "Sorry to be scaring y'all."

Ma flushed and gasped and stepped back. Pa opened up the door and let the ursavuul lumber in after him. He was a beast that walked like a man, covered in hair all over except for his big pale nose, which twitched at smells I couldn't smell. He wore a big black cloak full of bulging pockets. He moved in slowly and with a gentleness about his movements, like when you sneak up to a rabbit that you don't want to frighten off.

Pa sent the creature ahead into the kitchen, not knowing that's where I was hiding, while Ma yelled at him. She didn't try very hard to keep her voice down.

"What were you thinking, bringing that thing into our house?"

"He can hear you, Aster..."

"I don't give a damn if he can hear me. That thing is not welcome here."

The ursavuul didn't seem too fazed by the argument in the other room. He patted at his cloak pockets until he found a tiny iron kettle, which he filled with water and leaves and set up over our fire to boil. He had to bend his neck the whole time to keep from bonking it on the ceiling.

I was hiding behind the table, staring at the creature with wide eyes. I was not nearly so well hidden as I thought, as the ursavuul soon turned his small, dark eyes to meet mine. I startled, but the eyes crinkled kindly at me. They did not look like monstrous eyes at all.

"What's your name, little one?" the ursavuul asked me.

I would usually be offended at being called a little one—thirteen was already grown, as far as I was concerned—but, compared to the ursavuul, I was very little indeed. I was afraid to give him my name, because that was dangerous in some stories, so I didn't say anything at all.

"I understand being wary," the ursavuul said without a trace of judgment. "This is a dangerous part of the world."

When his kettle started to whistle, the ursavuul pinched its little handle and pulled it off from the hook above our fire. He poured steaming liquid into a cup that looked so dainty that I thought it must shatter in his claws, but he held it gently and blew on the surface before taking a sip. I noticed then that he didn't have claws at all, but only four furry fingers.

I bit my lip for a little strength over my fear, then inched out from my hiding place. His cup was full of green juice that smelled like flowers, even from where I was standing.

"What are you?" I asked.

"I am an ursavuul of the wandering tribe," he said amiably. "I travel all over the world, looking for treasures to bring home."

"Like saturnii," I said.

The mention of saturnii triggered a sudden and frightening transformation in the gentle giant. The ursavuul's hair raised up on his face, and his lips pulled back. "No," he growled. "Not like saturnii."

I flinched back into my hiding place and squeaked, "I'm sorry."

The ursavuul pulled back, pawing at the hair around his face in an attempt to brush the standing hairs back down. "I'm sorry," he apologized. "No, we bring things to Liander, God of Travels, in thanks for protecting us. Our true joy is in the traveling, you see, not the treasures. If I were a *saturniid*," he suddenly snarled again, with his lip flickering over his teeth. "I would *take* your treasures...or your eyes from your skull. I would not ask. I would not trade. I am *not* like them."

My father suddenly appeared behind me with a hand on my shoulder, summoned by his own paternal instinct. He squeezed me terribly hard while glaring at the giant.

"Daisy," he said to me, "Go fetch some of your lace to show the creature. Go on now." He pushed me around, interposing himself between me and the ursavuul.

I did as I was told. I brought over my pin-cushioned pillow with its work-in-progress flower on top. I struggled as I walked to keep my bobbins from knocking around and tangling up all the trailing threads. The beast pet at the flower's petals, marveling at their texture. The pupils of his eyes were so wide that there was hardly any brown left in them.

"It is singular, yes, this is perfect. Do you have more? I would see it all."

"Go get it all, Daisy," my mother urged, also taking a protective stance over me.

I brought down the box in which I stored all my projects that didn't have homes yet. There were tapered ribbons, experimental patterns in doilies, and projects where I'd snapped a thread but didn't want to undo the whole thing, so I just let it sit there unfinished until I had the heart to deconstruct it. All of it delighted the ursavuul, who received every piece with an animation that threatened to snap the wicker chair he sat upon.

"Beautiful, incredible, to see these things you can do with your tiny fingers. Look at this." He spread out his hand before me, which was bigger than my head, and had fingers the size of corn ears. "Do you think these fingers could ever make something this fine?"

I shook my head with a smile, charmed by his excitement. I ran back up and brought down my skirts and dresses where I'd hung lace off the cuffs or the neckline or the hem, or where I'd secured it overtop of fabric like embroidery. No one had ever shown so much delight in my passion, and I was overjoyed to share it with him. That was...until he announced that he wanted to "take it all."

"What?" I asked. "No, you can't have it!"

"Daisy," Pa rebuked, "behave yourself."

"But it's mine!"

"Go to your room."

"He can't take it." I tore away from my father and stuck my head under the ursavuul's big nose. "You won't take it."

"Daisy!" Pa pulled me away from the ursavuul, but I kept my eyes on it.

"You said you aren't a saturniid. You won't take it!"

Pa boxed my ear, filling my eyes with tears. "Room. Now."

"Now, now." The ursavuul's voice cut through the rest of our noise, as clear and deep as a bear's roar. He spoke to me. "Yes, as I told you, I don't take things for free. I will trade you for it, little one. As much as you can bear to part with."

I calmed a bit. "L-like what?"

"Well, I have rare stones," he drew out gemstones from one pocket. "And spices." He pulled out a little bottle of brown sand from another pocket. "I have dyes, which can make your threads any color of the rainbow. I have steel blades which will never rust. I have paper thinner than a feather, and books, if you know how to read. I have seeds from foreign plants. I have coins of gold and silver. And more." He pulled out examples from different pockets as he spoke, putting most of them right back where they came from. "Does any of that interest you?"

Cautiously, I nodded.

The ursavuul nodded back. "Then let us trade."

The ursavuul was clearly an experienced negotiator, but he had no intention of swindling us. I was protective of my favorite laces, and even though my childish stubbornness caused my parents a great deal of consternation, the ursavuul refused to make any deal until I'd agreed to it with enthusiasm. He ended up taking many of my abandoned works, because I let them go cheaply, and a few of my favorite things, because of how they showed off the best of my craft. I even begrudgingly gave away the skirt that I was wearing in exchange for a hoard of the powdered dyes, which I knew I could use to make even more beautiful things.

In the end, everyone left the table happy. My parents had new riches the likes of which had never been seen in our town: vials of sand whose fewest grains were enough to flavor a dish, gold and silver jewelry, and new boots of fine leather. The ursavuul had a bundle of new goods to add to his collection, which someone far away would doubtless find as magnificent to them as the other treasures had been to us. And I, well, I came away with my own gift, beyond anything tangible that the ursavuul had to offer, which I didn't come to appreciate until later. It was, put simply, a sense of value.

Before the ursavuul's wide back had disappeared over the hills, the details of his visit had already spread all over the town. This worldly creature thought that my lace was worth gold and silver, spices and dyes and fine leather, and that meant that it must be something special. Soon, everyone who was anyone had to have me make them something. My parents forgot their virtues of humility and simple work once my 'hobby' started earning them goods and social standing. Never again did my parents berate me for wasting time with weaving; so long as I was working on lace, they wouldn't make me get up and do any of my other chores at all. My parents had me make things for our household, things for the neighbors, things for everyone but me, and as soon as I was done with one project—no, before I was done—they would have another one ready for me to work on.

It got to be too much; they were too demanding. My hands cramped up and fell asleep, but when I told my parents that I couldn't work, they called me lazy. I acted out. I fought with them. One fight was so bad that Pa sent me out to sleep with the goats, because I was acting like a beast and not the girl he raised. Ma apologized afterwards and let me back in, but the damage was done, and I couldn't wait to move out of the house.

On my sixteenth birthday, we began negotiations for my betrothal. For a week and a half, I spent every night across the table from a different suitor and his family. They spoke to my parents over glasses of Ma's spiced cider while I sat in silence, weaving. Everything about these meetings–the cider, the lace tablecloth, the silent and obedient me–was meant to highlight my value. The whole process was wearying, but I enjoyed how it made my parents speak of me like they were proud. They said to look at how industrious and well-behaved and beautiful I was, even though they had always been faster to call me lazy and selfish. It was a little vindicating to hear them say the good things, even if they were used as tokens in a trade rather than freely given gifts.

I had to be silent during the negotiations because I was a strange girl, and it was better for me to appear mysterious and silent than to speak and reveal my strangeness. I didn't give flirts to my suitors any more than my parents gave compliments to me. I made myself cold to smiles and winks and jokes, knowing that I wasn't going to have much of a say, ultimately, in which of them I married. I was going to command a large bride price, and we were not a rich family. I was hopeful that whoever I married would let me go back to making things for myself, but not very hopeful. The people who would pay the highest for me were the ones who valued my gift the most, and if these past few years had taught me anything, that would mean less freedom rather than more. Little did I know.

Everyone on the ridge had at least one story of tragedy. Usually, the tragedies were consequences for breaking rules: going too far into the Mouth, going out at night, leaving candles lit in your windows, etc. I thought that I'd followed all the rules, but I forgot one: don't flaunt anything that a monster might want.

It was a night like any other. I woke with dread in the middle of the night to the sound of some scurrying on the roof. A squirrel on the run, perhaps. It was winter, and the shadows of a boney tree branch on my wall looked like the claw of a monster. In the wake of Colin's death, I had imagined this shadow as the 8-fingered hand of a froate. I was older now—too old to see monsters in shadows—but still I felt an unquenchable dread in my heart. I heard a click, like a twig tapping against the window down the hall, and I jumped with a childish gasp. I reprimanded myself—it was nothing—and pulled my blanket up to my chin, trying to think of anything other than monsters.

The image of a saturniid appeared in a silent flash in the middle of my doorframe. Her body may as well have been made of shadow, as it flickered in and out of moonlight like the windblown twigs of my shadow-tree. I blinked, trying to dispel this new apparition from my mind, and she jumped. Her wings unfurled. Red and gray and peach, they fanned out in an instant to display a pair of monstrous, yellow-rimmed eyes. These slowed her descent so that she landed upon the foot of my bed with a light step that caused not even a creak. Her feet ended in hawkish talons, which pierced through my sheets as though the bed were made of butter, leaving a trail of tears where she stepped. Her eye-patterned wings furled back in silence, balancing her out as she leaned over me. Her face was white and featureless, with neither nose nor mouth, but only a pair of black, orb-shaped eyes. The white fur of her face was soaked in parts with wet blood. The rust-red outlined a crease that ran up the middle of her face, all the way from chin to brow. When her white face opened, it first fell forward like a drawbridge, then the crease split, and out rolled a long black tendril of a tongue, as long as an arm and ending in a four-pronged set of feelers. It touched me on my face, gently, slimy, as I seized up in terror.

The saturniid reached down with a clawed hand, past my neck, to the lace frill on my pillow beside me. She held the lace up in front of me. Then pointed, and gestured, in a jagged imitation of the shurtles' unspoken hand-language, *Is this you?*

"Wh-What are you—" I whispered, but as I spoke, the creature jabbed her claw into my mouth, and pierced my tongue through both the top and bottom. She ripped out, like she intended to take my tongue wholly from my mouth and fling it into the wall, but her grip wasn't strong enough, so she only cut twin gashes through the flash and spattered blood on my lace.

I covered my mouth with my hands to keep from screaming out. The pain brought clarity. She wasn't an apparition: she was really here. She didn't like noise.

You make that? The creature signed, stabbing a bloody claw into my pillow.

I nodded in affirmation.

The saturniid wore strips of studded leather wound around her torso and upper legs, with belted-down pouches for holding treasures. She opened one of these pouches to show me a bloodstained piece of cloth.

You make this? she asked me.

I swallowed the blood that filled my mouth, then unfolded the tattered parcel. It was a periwinkle skirt, with a lacy image of a girl sitting on a hill. Tears welled in my eyes as I thought of what must have happened to the gentle ursavuul who'd carried it, the first being ever to appreciate my lace as I did. I nodded again, struggling not to make an audible sniff lest the creature spear my nose next.

My father lit a lantern down the hall, and its distant light made the creature turn around suddenly. She leaped from my bed as a silent shadow and drifted down behind the doorframe. I wanted to yell out, but was paralyzed to silence as the light drew closer, and eventually rounded the doorway.

The creature struck out with one of its talons at my father's neck, cutting into it in three places. While his lantern fell, she squeezed my father's neck, snapped through his spine, and then caught the lantern before it could hit the ground. He couldn't scream, but only made a ghastly gurgle-wheeze in his crushed throat as the saturniid lowered him to the ground. His eyes were wide with terror for the few moments before he died, as the monster opened her hinge-mouth, unfurled her proboscis-tendril, and wrapped the four-pronged feelers around one of his eyes. She squeezed and pulled and snapped its tether. The tendril wrapped itself back up, bringing the eye to her unhinged mouth. She chewed on the eyeball, then unfurled again and repeated with the other. The last thing that my father saw before he died was the four-pronged feeler, and then darkness.

I couldn't talk or move. I watched him die. I didn't do anything. I couldn't even cry.

After what felt like an eternity, the saturniid turned her attention back to me.

You come with me, she signed. *Bring that.* She gestured at the thread, bobbins, and lace that I had been working with.

I stood up out of my bed, though I shook terribly and felt faint. It was cold, and I shivered in my nightdress. My two little brothers shared a room with me, but they hadn't awoken. I was grateful that they slept deeply; I think that if they had so much as spoken in their sleep, they too would be dead.

Where? I signed, though I stumbled to follow her directions.

Home, she signed back. *You are mine now.*

Home could only mean one place: Myriid, deep in the Monsters' Mouth. It was a place from stories, a warning to children: don't be bad or you'll be taken to Myriid and strung up some place in the saturnii's boasting exhibits of pilfered treasures.

I wrapped all of my lacing supplies up in a blanket, extra careful not to disturb my brothers into waking. I followed the saturniid out of my bedroom, stepping over my father and the puddle of his blood. I glanced to my right as I left, towards my parents' room.

Ma stood in the hall, wide-eyed and silent.

I did not scream at her. She did not scream at me. Both choices together saved her life, as the creature kept walking forward, out the door, into the night. My eyes filled with tears as I stared at my mother.

I couldn't tell her I loved her, or I was sorry, or even goodbye, lest the eye-eater take notice and make a second meal of her. I closed my eyes and wiped my nose and followed the monster outside.

It was a clear, cold night. The grass was lush gray in the moonlight, and swayed with the wind. There was some commotion down the way at another farmhouse, where a shouting crowd gathered with torches and weapons. I suspected that my house hadn't been the first one that the eye-eater visited that night.

The saturniid gestured to me, *Hold that.*

I hugged my bundle close to my chest. The saturniid unfurled its wings, jumped, and landed on me. Her talons pierced painfully into my shoulders as she took hold and leaped up from the ground with me hanging like a rag-doll underneath her. Wind rushed past us. She flew across the hillside, down into the sunflower valley, then further, deeper, down into the Monsters' Mouth.

Milton Keynes UK
Ingram Content Group UK Ltd.
UKHW022107190224
438095UK00017B/708